## "The stalker you're running from is here in Florida, Melissa," Chris said.

The color leached from her face, and she sagged against the side of the car, clutching her stomach and shaking her head in denial. "No, he couldn't have found me. I was so careful."

The fear in those wide blue eyes snagged his heart, and at that moment he would have done anything to make it go away. But he didn't want to give her false security. "It could be nothing. I didn't want to worry you, but I had to let you know."

She didn't respond.

"Melissa," he whispered. He rested his hand lightly on her forearm and took the box from her. "I'm here for you, Missy. Let me help."

She turned slowly to face him. Tears threatened to pool on her lower lashes, but she blinked them away. She was trying so hard to be strong.

"Nobody expects you to do this alone. Please let me help."

She gave two brief nods.

### CAROL J. POST

From medical secretary to court reporter to property manager to owner of a special events decorating company, Carol's resumé reads like someone who doesn't know what she wants to be when she grows up. But one thing that has remained constant through the years is her love for writing. She started as a child writing poetry for family and friends, then graduated to articles which actually made it into some religious and children's publications. Several years ago (more than she's willing to admit), she penned her first novel. In 2010, she decided to get serious about writing fiction for publication and joined Romance Writers of America, Tampa Area Romance Authors and Faith, Hope & Love, RWA's online inspirational chapter. She has placed in numerous writing contests, including RWA's 2012 Golden Heart®.

Carol lives in sunshiny central Florida with her husband (who is her own real-life hero) and writes her stories under the shade of the oaks in her yard. She holds a bachelor's degree in business and professional leadership, which doesn't contribute much to writing fiction but helps a whole lot in the business end of things. Besides writing, she works alongside her music minister husband singing and playing the piano. She also enjoys sailing, hiking, camping—almost anything outdoors. Her two grown daughters and grandson live too far away for her liking, so she now pours all that nurturing into taking care of three fat and sassy cats and one highly spoiled dog.

# MIDNIGHT SHADOWS

## CAROL J. POST

*Love Inspired*

Recycling programs
for this product may
not exist in your area.

™ LOVE INSPIRED BOOKS

ISBN-13: 978-0-373-67544-9

MIDNIGHT SHADOWS

www.LoveInspiredBooks.com

**Printed in U.S.A.**

Not a single sparrow can fall to the ground without your Father knowing it. And the very hairs on your head are all numbered.
—*Matthew* 10:29b–30

This book is dedicated to my husband, Chris,
the inspiration for every hero I create.
I'm so glad you never stopped believing in me.

Thank you to my family, Kristi, Andrea, Kim,
Jerry, Mom Roberts and Mom Post. All these years
you've encouraged me to keep the dream alive.

Many thanks to all my writing buddies—
my awesome critique partners, Karen Fleming and
Dixie Taylor, whose input has been invaluable,
and my fellow TARANs (Tampa Area Romance
Authors), without whose support I couldn't have
done it. And thank you to my friends Jeri Del Ross,
Renate Malcolm and Kristen Harris,
who never get tired of reading my stories.

And a huge thank you to my lovely editor,
Rachel Burkot, who saw potential in me
and gave me this opportunity to do what I love.
You are beyond awesome!

# PROLOGUE

Jagged streaks danced across the night sky, bathing the landscape in harsh white light.

Crouched behind the old sedan, Melissa Langston cringed. Each burst of virtual daylight shredded her already frayed nerves. She needed the cover of darkness.

A clap resonated through the air and gave way to a deep, persistent rumble. In the silence that followed, she tuned her ear to the dull thump of muffled footsteps, straining to pinpoint their source. Why couldn't he wear boots? The hard soles would at least warn her if he veered from the sidewalk.

But Eugene always wore tennis shoes.

She held her breath, every muscle a tangled knot of apprehension. He was suspicious. But he hadn't seen her. She was sure of it. Otherwise, he would have come after her.

His sudden appearance had almost sent her into cardiac arrest. She had slipped from her apartment for the final time and just reached the parking lot when movement at the end of the building caught her eye. A split second later, she dove behind the nearest car. That was almost an hour ago, when the approaching spring storm was nothing more than distant heat lightning and a vague threat of rain.

Another series of flashes illuminated the sky, and she counted. One thousand one, one thousand two... The ground trembled beneath her. Almost eight seconds. A mile and a half away. The rain was even closer, its musty, organic scent heavy in the air.

But it wasn't the rain that worried her. It was the lightning.

And Eugene.

The last time she checked, he still paced back and forth in front of her apartment. The restraining order she filed several weeks ago was little consolation. So was the thought that help was minutes away. Her phone was in her purse, waiting in the console of her car. But if Eugene saw her run for it, she wouldn't have the opportunity to dial nine-one-one. He had warned her. She could never leave, or she would regret it. If the ice-cold fury in his eyes didn't convince her, the steel blade against her throat did.

Anger surged up from within, nudging aside a sliver of the fear. She didn't ask for this. How could friendly conversation on laundry night and the occasional visit to the ice cream shop across the street morph into this sick obsession that left her fleeing for her life?

A liquid trail of silver fire zigzagged downward, followed by an answering clap. Then a deathly silence settled in. The footsteps had stopped. *Where was Eugene?* Awareness zinged up her spine, and she tensed, every sense on full alert. He was close. She could feel it.

She dropped to all fours and crawled along the length of the back bumper, the roughness of the asphalt against her hands and knees an annoying undertone to the alarms going off in her head. Her heart beat a staccato rhythm in her chest, and she paused to draw in a steadying breath. The instant she peered around the side of the car, another flash pierced the darkness, and a wave of panic cascaded over her. Eugene stood at the front quarter panel, not twelve feet away.

She drew back and pivoted on one leg, grinding the skin from her bare knee, and then scurried to the other side of the car.

An earsplitting boom accompanied the next flash, and she bit off a startled shriek. Had he seen her? Even if he hadn't, he could step around the old sedan at any moment and stumble upon her carelessly chosen hiding place. Then he would know she was leaving.

And she would pay with her life.

Dread settled over her, seeping into her pores and filling her limbs with lead. But she had no choice. Talking to him had accomplished nothing. Threatening him with a restraining order only made him mad. And *getting* the restraining order triggered a fit of rage that left her pinned against the laundry room wall with a knife at her throat. Even the police had been no help. By the time they arrived, Eugene was always gone. No, running was her only hope.

She sat back on her heels, again in a deep squat. Molten lava coursed through her knee with every beat of her heart. She reached to brush away the embedded grains of sand and gravel, wet and sticky with her own blood, and dropped her hand. She would doctor herself later. Ignoring the fire raging in her knee, she raised herself to peer through the windows of the old sedan. *Where was he?*

With the next brilliant flash, she knew. He stood at her Honda two spaces over, bent at the waist, peering inside.

Thankfully, the last of her things had fit in the trunk. A backseat filled with boxes would have sealed her fate. This was her fourth—and final—midnight trip. Her cat waited at a friend's house. Everything else was packed into a rented box truck in her friend's driveway. Freedom was so close, she could almost taste it.

A whispered "shhhh" sounded in the distance and moved steadily closer, building to a rumble then a roar as thousands of advancing minisoldiers pounded across the parking lot. The next instant, she was drenched. Rain tainted with hair spray, moisturizer and makeup trailed down her forehead and into her eyes. The sting competed with the pain in her knee.

She wiped her face with her soaked shirt and searched for Eugene's stocky frame. Several seconds passed before she spotted him. He had moved away from her car and strolled down the sidewalk, seemingly unperturbed by the hammering rain. Even after his retreating figure disappeared from view, she remained in her semicrouch, unable to shake the feeling that just when she reached her car, meaty fingers would clamp around her throat.

She finally summoned the courage to emerge from her hiding place and closed the final yards at a sprint, prodded by urgency with an edge of panic. The panic grew, pounded up her spine and pressed on her chest. With shaking fingers, she jammed the key into the lock.

Light flooded the interior of the car, and she shot a glance back at the building, half expecting Eugene to materialize there. When he didn't, she slipped into the seat and slammed the door, eyes still glued to the point where the shadows had swallowed him earlier. She reached for her phone, navigating the three numbers with her thumb. She had placed dozens of these calls. And each time it was pointless. Eugene had a knack for disappearing into thin air. Maybe it was his military training. Maybe he had given her a false name right from the start, and that was why there was no record of him, military or otherwise. It was as if he didn't exist.

Much later, she sped through the darkness down Interstate 75, the Honda attached securely to the back of the truck and Smudge in a carrier beside her. Layer by layer, her tension peeled away, falling off with every mile that rolled by, and relief settled in, mixed with a sort of wry humor. She had done it. She had escaped. She was starting over—a new home, a new job, a new name and a new life.

But she was doing the one thing she swore she would never do.

Going home.

# ONE

It was the kind of day that made her wish she had kept hitting the snooze button.

One of the worst since returning to Harmony Grove four months ago. Nothing catastrophic—no earthquakes or hurricanes or even small house fires. Her escape-artist cat was recaptured and locked safely inside, she had plenty of bread to replace the two burnt slices, and her clothes had finally dried after her sprint into her office through pouring rain. Just lots of minor annoyances that had a way of ruining a person's day.

But it was almost over. One more deposition and she could go home, provided the roof didn't fall in.

Melissa took a seat at the end of the table and began to set up her steno machine. Then her gaze dropped to the deposition notice, and she froze, one hand on the tripod and the other sprawled across the top of the machine.

Christopher Jamison.

The roof *could* have fallen in at that moment. She probably wouldn't have noticed.

She stared at the name and wrestled in a breath through constricted airways. The vise that gripped her heart was painfully familiar. So was the bitterness gnawing a hole in her gut. But that was ancient history. She had conquered any stray feelings for Chris Jamison, beating them into submission until they retreated, cowering, to some dark, untouched corner of her heart. When that hadn't worked, she had shoved them aside with frenzied activity.

Her eyes swept over the name again. It couldn't be the same Chris Jamison. *Hers* had left Florida five years ago, with no intention of coming back. Of course, so had she. Life had a way of disrupting the best of plans.

Two attorneys entered, and when the buzzer on the conference room phone sounded, Attorney Daniels held the receiver to his ear. "Great. I'll meet him at the top of the stairs."

Her heart jumped to double time, and a sudden sheet of moisture coated her palms. There weren't many names on her People-I-Hope-to-Never-See-Again list, but Chris Jamison's was right near the top. She wiped her hands on her skirt, then brushed imaginary specks from the lacquered mahogany conference table. Moments later, voices drifted into the room.

"Mr. Jamison? I'm Jonathan Daniels."

"Chris Jamison. Sorry I'm late. The Friday afternoon traffic was worse than I expected."

*Oh, no, it's him!* That smooth, rich baritone was

unmistakable. A bolt of panic shot through her, and she glanced wildly around the room, looking for a way of escape. There was the open door, with Mr. Daniels and his witness just outside, and the window directly behind her. An image sprang to mind—a heel-clad reporter climbing through the opening and plopping unceremoniously into the bushes below—and the panic threatened to give way to hysterical laughter. She struggled to compose herself. Any second he would walk through the door.

Her hands flew to her hair, which wasn't likely to go anywhere. It was pulled into a French braid and secured with a silver clip, an emergency purchase after her rain fiasco. And her skirt and jacket were fine. She resisted the urge to straighten them and willed her body to relax. If she couldn't feel confident, she could at least look it.

No amount of willpower, however, could prepare her for the moment he stepped inside. Five long years slipped away in an instant, and every sweet moment they had ever shared crashed back on her in one massive wave.

Little had changed. He had obviously kept up his gym membership—the pale blue sports shirt and dark dress jeans couldn't camouflage the rock-hard body beneath. And his sandy-blond hair was as thick as ever, an irresistible mix of styled good taste and wind-swept charm. He stood with one thumb hooked into his jeans pocket, the epitome of confidence, making her loss of composure feel that much more complete.

"And," Mr. Daniels continued, "this is Melissa Morris, our court reporter."

Chris started to nod, then froze midgreeting. His dark eyes registered recognition, then denial, realization and finally shock. His lower jaw went slack, and he stared at her in wide-eyed silence. Seeing him so befuddled boosted her own sagging confidence, and she was again struck with an irrational urge to laugh. She squelched the urge, but couldn't conquer the grin quivering at the corners of her mouth.

He recovered all too quickly. Hardness crept into his gaze, and he acknowledged her with a curt nod. "Pleased to meet you."

The lie rolled easily off his tongue. But a muscle twitched in his lower jaw, calling him out. He was anything but pleased.

Mr. Daniels indicated the chair next to her. "Have a seat, and we'll get this over with."

She jerked her gaze away from Chris to the attorney. His words seemed oddly out of place. How could life continue uninterrupted when her whole world had been turned upside down?

She nodded and gathered her scattered thoughts. Those eyes once again settled on her, dark and brooding. What was his problem? After all, he was the one who had withheld his trust and made ridiculous accusations. But she was the one who had walked in on every woman's worst nightmare. And the one left with the distasteful job of "uninviting" 175 guests to a wedding that would never take place.

"Raise your right hand, please." As soon as she began to administer the oath, she got tongue-tied. Her mouth didn't want to cooperate. The pleasant aroma of her after-lunch breath mint was long gone, replaced by a distinct flavor of metal, as if she had chewed and swallowed a box of nails. She shot a prayer heavenward and tried again, this time successful.

Mr. Daniels began his questioning. "State your name for the record, please."

"Christopher Wayne Jamison."

"What is your residence address?"

She stopped, fingers suspended over the keys. Lakeland! What was he doing in central Florida?

The deposition continued—question, answer, question, answer—and she skillfully recorded every word. He was in Florida temporarily running his father's marine store, on leave from the Memphis Police Department, which meant he wasn't going to stay. He had visited a year earlier and witnessed the defendant run a red light and slam into the plaintiff. And he remembered the defendant appeared intoxicated, an observation that drew an objection from Mr. Edwards, attorney for the defense.

But the answers she really wanted wouldn't come out in testimony. Namely, did his life turn out as he had hoped, or did he kick himself for the choices he had made? Had she invaded his thoughts as much as he had hers over the past five years? And why did he blame her for what went wrong between them, when he was the one who messed up?

Mr. Daniels finished his questioning, and Attorney Edwards began his cross-examination. Thank goodness, it was almost over. Sitting next to Chris for the past thirty minutes was like slowly tearing the scab from a wound, which made no sense. Any wounds he had inflicted had long since healed over. At least she thought they had. It was easy to convince herself she was over him when he was three hundred miles away.

"No further questions." Mr. Edwards laid down his pen.

A familiar uneasiness crept over her, that hollow-gut-compressed-chest sensation she used to get before a presentation or big test. *Lord, please don't make me have to talk to him.* She hauled in a stabilizing breath. If she took her time packing up her equipment, Chris would be gone before she reached the parking lot.

Or not. Mr. Daniels addressed him. "How's the marine business?"

"Pretty busy, actually, in spite of the poor economy."

"Glad to hear it. I'm a regular customer of yours. I've been restoring an old Chris-Craft, so Jamison Marine has become a regular entry on my credit card statements. You know the definition of a boat—a hole in the water you throw money into."

Chris laughed. "You got that right. 'Boat' is an

acronym. It stands for 'break out another thousand.'"
He leaned back in his chair, lips curved into a relaxed smile, warm and friendly. That smile wasn't
for her. But her heart answered with an unexpected
flutter anyway.

She dropped her gaze and slid her steno machine
into its case. *Keep talking.* It didn't matter who left
first, as long as they didn't leave together. If she got
her equipment packed up quickly enough, he would
still be knee-deep in boat talk.

That wasn't unusual for Chris—both the topic and
the ease of conversation. He had that smooth, simple
manner that encouraged openness, even from total
strangers. And a smile that could charm the slip-
pers right off an ice princess. But she wasn't going
to think about that.

Soon her notice, pen and tape recorder were tucked
away, along with the steno machine. And that was the
moment the conversation died. Chris stood to leave,
and because she had no other choice, she did, too.

He followed her into the hall. "I thought you were
living in Atlanta."

"And I thought you were in Tennessee."

"I was till three weeks ago. My dad died suddenly,
so I came back to wrap things up."

"I'm sorry." She really was. "I didn't know."

"It was unexpected. He was fine one minute, dead
of a heart attack the next."

He swung open the heavy oak door and held it for
her. The instant she stepped through, a wall of heat

and humidity pressed into her, sucking the air from her lungs. The day's sporadic rain showers had finally stopped, and the sun was out full force, transforming the parking lot into a concrete sauna. She sucked in a steamy breath. Fall was less than two weeks away. But someone forgot to tell Florida.

He let the door swing shut. "I've taken a three-month leave of absence from the force, but hopefully it won't take that long to find a buyer for the house and store."

"I see." She unclipped her keys from the D-ring on the side of her purse and started across the parking lot. Azaleas blazed hot-fuchsia against a white vinyl fence, and palm trees stood at attention, fronds waving lazily in a gentle breeze, whispering that all was right with the world. The scene was deceptively serene. At the moment, her world was anything but.

"How long have you been back?" he asked.

"Four months." *Plus one week and three days.* And she still hadn't stopped looking over her shoulder. Eugene didn't know where she had gone. He had no idea where "home" was or that she had changed her name. She even got her mail at a post office box in another town. But none of those precautions took away the nightmares or brought back her former carefree life.

Chris cleared his throat and pulled his own keys from his pocket. "So when did you get married?"

She looked at him sharply. "Huh?"

"Morris?"

"Oh, that." She shrugged. "I'm not married."

He arched one brow and tilted his head in silent question—one she left unanswered.

"So what brought you back?" he asked.

"Some friends got transferred and didn't want to leave the house vacant." Of course, there was more to it than that. Being given use of the Tylers' four-bedroom, three-bath house on five acres for nothing more than upkeep and utilities costs was tempting enough. But when the offer came right when she was planning her escape from Atlanta, that clinched it.

His brows again arched upward. "And you picked up and moved from another state just to help them out? That's pretty generous of you."

"It was time for a change." She opened her passenger door and put her equipment on the seat. When she turned back around, he stood studying her with those probing eyes. She closed her door and brushed past him. He could save his detective work for the Memphis P.D. She didn't need his help.

He followed her around to the driver's side. "Take it easy."

"You, too." She opened her door and slid into the seat. "I'm sorry about your father. I hope it all goes well for you, getting the store sold and everything."

"Thank you." He closed her door and dipped his head in farewell. His eyes glinted golden in the fading afternoon sun, stirring to life embers long since burned out, and she fought against the effect. After all that had happened between them, she shouldn't feel anything except bitterness.

As she started the car and put it in Reverse, a scene flashed into her mind, so vivid she wanted to retch—Chris in the arms of her best friend. Oh, yes, the bitterness was still there. One didn't easily forget that kind of betrayal.

*Forgive us our debts as we forgive our debtors.*

The verse intruded unexpectedly, and she reached for the radio dial, pushing the thought aside. Soft rock filled the car, some seventies love song written long before she was born. She focused on the words, clinging to the distraction they offered. It didn't help.

*Forgive us our debts as we forgive our debtors.*

After only three months in the faith, she was no scholar. But she had a nagging suspicion that "debtors" might somehow include Chris. What exactly did God expect?

*I don't hate him. Isn't that good enough?*

A gentle nudge told her it wasn't.

The traffic light ahead turned yellow, and she eased to a stop. Moments later, deep bass rattled her windows and reverberated in her chest. She glanced at the rusted Dodge next to her and reached for her own radio dial. Blaring music wasn't such a bad idea. Anything to drown out that nudge that wasn't so gentle anymore.

She didn't want to listen to that still, small voice. In fact, she wanted to leave God out of the whole situation. Because if she asked in earnest, He would probably give her an answer, one she didn't want to hear. He would likely demand that she let go of the past and forgive the unforgivable.

And she just wasn't ready.

Chris pulled from the parking lot, following the same route Melissa had taken. Except his would end a few blocks down, at the Lakeland home where he grew up. Since his return, he had avoided the little town of Harmony Grove, some thirty minutes away. And tonight was no exception. Even more so now that Melissa was back.

Walking into that attorney's office and seeing her sitting there had left him reeling. That was a part of his life he had neatly bundled up and locked away. Maybe if he could have had some warning, some time to prepare… Who was he kidding? Facing Melissa again would have knocked the foundation out from under him no matter how much advance notice he got.

Five years ago, she'd broken his heart. For two years he hated her. Then he found out how wrong he'd been.

And he'd spent the next two years hating himself.

He shouldn't have doubted her. He should have believed her when she insisted there was nothing between her and her ex-boyfriend Lance. But the signs were there—plans postponed because "something came up," a stream of excuses for why she was late. And her best friend only fed that doubt. But Adrianne had an agenda. He'd just been too naive to see it. So when she told him Melissa had reignited sparks with her high school sweetheart, he believed her. That was *his* mistake.

But Melissa had thrown it all away so easily. She hadn't loved him enough to fight for what they had. And that was *her* mistake.

He pressed the brake and eased to a stop in front of the double garage door. Inside was his dad's Cadillac…along with fifty-five years of life. So until he got around to cleaning out the garage, his Blazer would remain in the driveway.

He stepped from the vehicle with a sigh. As much as he wanted to just push Melissa from his mind, as a cop, there were alarms he couldn't ignore. She was in trouble, and it was taking its toll. Oh, she looked as good as ever, with that thick, dark hair that went halfway down her back, even when braided, and those expressive blue eyes. But worry marked her features, and an undercurrent of tension flowed just beneath the surface, evidence of a constant state of being on guard. Even though she did her best to hide it, she was afraid of something.

What kind of trouble had she found? Or a more accurate question would be, "What kind of trouble had found her?" Melissa was a by-the-book kind of girl, not likely to end up on the wrong side of the law. But she was running from something. She'd changed her name and abruptly left Atlanta. Maybe she'd witnessed a crime. Or maybe she was trying to escape some psycho ex-boyfriend.

Whatever it was, it wasn't his problem. He was off duty, on leave of absence from police work for three whole months. He didn't need to concern himself with whatever mess Melissa had gotten into. Harmony Grove had police officers. Let someone else worry about her. Someone who could do his job and not make it personal. That someone wasn't him.

But he couldn't let it go that easily. He had to know what she was up against. Tonight he would call his partner and have him pull up everything he could find on both names—Melissa Langston and Melissa Morris. What he would do with the information, he had no idea. But at least he would know.

He jammed the key into the lock and swung the front door inward. Inside the house, his father's presence was everywhere, from his favorite afghan draped over the back of the recliner, to the World War II titles lining the bookshelves, to the stale, sweet scent of his pipe. A wave of loneliness washed over him, shot though with a pang of guilt. In the past five years, he'd been back only twice—once last year and once the year before that. He shouldn't have stayed away so long. Weekly calls just weren't the same as visits.

The ringtone sounded on his phone, and he pulled it from its pouch, thankful for the distraction. It was Roger Tandy, longtime friend and one of Jamison Marine's best customers.

"I called the store, and they gave me your cell number," Roger began. "I'd like you to come and take a look at my boat. I'm thinking of having you sell it on consignment."

He agreed, because he really had no choice, and set it up for Monday afternoon, all the while wishing Roger would just bring the boat to him. The thirty-minute drive was no problem. The fact that the Tandys lived in Harmony Grove was. It was a quaint, pretty town right off the set of some fifties movie, with nostalgic shops, a park at its center and people who actually stopped to chat. At one time, it was a place of magic, where love bloomed and dreams came true. Then in a brief instant, it became the embodiment of everything he had lost.

For three weeks he had avoided it.

Maybe it was time to face his demons.

# TWO

Melissa eased to a stop, doing her best not to grimace. With the windows up and the A/C on, though, a prolonged groan was probably safe. Carolyn Platt stood on the sidewalk in front of Beth-Ann's Fabric and Craft Shoppe, squinting in the afternoon sun and waving frantically. As much as Melissa wanted to keep driving, she was stuck—she had already made eye contact. She lowered the window and Carolyn waddled into the street, platinum curls piled high atop her head.

"Melissa, dear, I'm so glad I caught you. Guess who I saw drive past not ten minutes ago, headed toward your place, I might add."

"I have no idea."

"Don't you?" Carolyn waggled her brows, something she always did when poised to collect or disseminate some juicy gossip. "It was Chris."

"Well, I can assure you, he's not here to see me."

Carolyn nodded her head. "Mmm-hmm." But neither the nod nor the murmur fooled Melissa. Carolyn was busy planning how she was going to spread this newest juicy tidbit. It wouldn't be difficult. In Harmony Grove, gossip flowed like water down a steep slope.

Melissa started to ease off the brake and roll forward, but Carolyn's hand on the open window stopped her.

"I actually flagged you down to see if you would make some of your mother's cookies for the Busy Bees Bake Sale next Saturday. We could really use some of those famous Langston double chocolate chip cookies. Even though you're not a Langston anymore."

Melissa smiled, ignoring the jab. All Carolyn knew was that she came back with a different last name and no husband. No amount of dropping hints had given her the information she wanted. And it was killing her. "I'll be happy to. So who's getting the proceeds this time?"

"This year we're helping the Polk Shelter for Abused Women and Children. They're trying to expand their facilities."

"Glad I can help."

Each fall, the Busy Bees Quilting Circle held a huge bake sale at Harmony Grove's arts and crafts show and donated the money to a different charitable cause. The amount was nothing to sneeze at—people came from all over the county, thanks to full-page ads in every newspaper within a fifty-mile radius, all generously funded by Dr. Stephens.

"I'll get those cookies baked," she promised, starting to ease forward. But Carolyn waylaid her once again.

"How is your mother, by the way?"

*A mess. Still searching for something she's unlikely to find. At least where she's looking.* But she would never tell Carolyn that. "Mom's fine." The words were partially true. She was in good health, and her current man seemed to be taking better care of her than her last ones had.

Carolyn nodded and dropped her hand. "Well, I don't want to hold you up. Thank you for the cookies."

"No problem," she responded, but Carolyn had already turned her back and was hurrying toward the opposite sidewalk. She got around extremely well, considering her girth and her age—whatever that was. No one knew for sure. It was the best-kept secret in Harmony Grove. Actually, it was the *only* secret in Harmony Grove, thanks to Carolyn.

When Melissa reached the end of Shadowood Lane, the long gravel driveway was empty. Disappointment settled over her, and she silently scolded herself. Regardless of what Carolyn said, she didn't really expect him to be there. And she didn't *want* him to be there. Eventually he would head back to Memphis. In the meantime, the less she saw of him the better.

She stopped next to the house and walked the path she had just driven. Monday was trash collection day, and the big green can waited for her at the end of the driveway. It was a long trek—the house was far from neighbors on either side. Maybe one day she would appreciate the privacy. That day seemed light years away.

She grasped the handle and began wheeling the can back up the gravel drive. In another life, the setting would feel like paradise. Colorful flower beds flowed into one another in graceful curves, and in their midst, the two-story house stood majestic and proud with its columned porch and cheery red front door. All around, a gentle breeze whispered through the massive oaks, compelling the world to be still and listen.

But one quality stood out more than all the others—seclusion, that sense of total aloneness. And it was anything but comforting.

She rounded the back corner of the house, ready to deposit the trash can in its usual spot on the patio. When her gaze slid past the kitchen door to the span of wall beyond, an icy blade of fear slashed through her.

The family room window was shattered. Someone had broken into the house.

For several moments, she stood frozen. Her brain shouted orders to run. But her leaden limbs wouldn't cooperate.

Eugene couldn't have found her. Not so soon. *Dear God, please, no.*

The wind picked up, rustling the branches overhead, and as if on command, crickets came to life, their song a warning, filling the air around her. She stood frozen, praying she was alone but wishing to God she wasn't. She couldn't go into the house.

Her car beckoned, and she fought the urge to get in and drive, to leave Harmony Grove far behind and not stop until she found somewhere safe. If such a place existed. But she didn't start the car. Instead, she pulled her cell phone from her purse. Maybe it was nothing more than vandalism, or someone looking for quick cash. But she wasn't budging until she saw flashing blue-and-red lights.

Minutes later, a Harmony Grove police car pulled in behind her. The driver's door opened, and a familiar figure unfolded and straightened to his full height. It was Alan, Adrianne's little brother. She stepped from the car and waved a greeting. She couldn't hold him accountable for the sins of his sister.

"You reported a break-in?"

"Yes, I did. They broke a window." She led him around the side of the house and past the back patio— next to a good-sized limb. She had been so focused on the window, she hadn't seen it.

Alan noticed it, too. "How long has this limb been down?"

"I don't know. I didn't see it until now."

He picked up one end of the branch. "It seems as if it would have hit the roof overhang rather than the window, but I suppose it's possible, especially if it got hung up on the way down." While he dragged the limb away from the house, she stepped up to the window. Miniblinds swayed gently behind a fist-size hole, and jagged shards of glass littered the wooden sill, more inside than out.

Alan picked up one of the larger pieces and laid it back on the sill. "Anything missing?"

Embarrassment crept over her. Why didn't she notice the limb before she called the police? "Uh... I haven't checked."

"It's okay." He smiled his understanding. "We'll go in together."

She unlocked the back door and followed him inside. His broad shoulders filled out the uniform well—she was still trying to get used to the transformation. When she left, he was a scrawny fifteen-year-old that looked like a brisk wind might carry him away. Now he was quite the protector, striking in navy blue, a pistol at his hip. It was amazing what a growth spurt, a set of weights and a stint in the police academy could do.

He walked into each room ahead of her and waited while she searched. Nothing appeared disturbed. In the family room, several shards of glass had found their way through the blinds and onto the back of the couch, but most of it lay on the windowsill. Some of the slats had been left cockeyed, no doubt shuffled by the end of the branch.

She climbed the stairs, and when she walked into the master bedroom, her pulse began to race. The large walk-in closet held everything of value that she owned. She swung open the wooden bifold doors.

Her camera bag sat untouched on the shelf, and her laptop stood against the built-in shoe rack. Two rows of necklaces hung on vinyl-covered pegs, cut glass and semiprecious stones glittering under the overhead light. Inside the drawers of her jewelry box, the rings, bracelets and earrings lay just as she had left them. Nothing was missing.

She heaved a sigh of relief and turned toward Alan, who waited patiently in the doorway. "Nothing's been touched. I guess I've only been invaded by a tree branch." She smiled sheepishly. "Sorry I bothered you."

"You didn't bother me." A teasing grin curved his mouth, reminding her of the mischievous little brother who was forever crashing her, BethAnn and Adrianne's activities. "You just spared me from another boring afternoon. This is the first excitement I've had since old Harry Jones thought his car got stolen last week." He turned to walk from the room and continued talking over one shoulder. "We ended up finding it at C.J.'s Garage. He forgot he had taken it in for service."

Melissa laughed. "It's scary he still lives alone."

She followed him down the stairs, then stopped suddenly. Smudge didn't meet her at the door. And he wasn't in any of his usual spots. "I haven't seen my cat."

"He's probably hiding. I imagine breaking glass would scare a cat half to death."

Probably so. But loud noises don't scare deaf cats.

A familiar uneasiness settled over her, that ever-present sense of being on edge. It waxed and waned but never disappeared.

Alan studied her for several moments. "Do you need help with the window?"

"Thanks, but you're on duty. I'll just nail up a board for tonight and call Handy Andy tomorrow."

"Are you sure? I don't mind."

He didn't, but his chief would. "I'm sure. You get back to your police duties, and I'll take care of the window."

She could handle it. She was used to taking care of herself. She had been alone for five years. But even before then—before she left Harmony Grove and her mom sold the house and left, too—she was alone. For almost as long as she could remember, she had been alone.

And it was starting to get old.

Marge Tandy followed Chris onto her front porch. She had just conned him into helping her at the arts and crafts show, and he wasn't even sure how it had happened. Sure, Roger was going to be away on a business trip, but there had to be someone who could help set up her canopy and display her paintings.

But she had begged, and he didn't have a valid excuse—Derrick and Sam really could man the store without him. One look at those pleading eyes, and he was a goner—the word *no* fled his vocabulary.

But that was nothing new when Marge was involved. His dealings with the Tandys went back four-teen years, when they bought their first boat from Jamison Marine. He was fifteen, working in his father's store after school. His dad and Roger became fast friends, and Marge became the mother he never had.

She pulled the door shut behind her and smiled up at him. "I'm sorry about the circumstances that brought you here, but I'm glad you're back. This is where you belong."

"Actually, I'm not staying. I'm planning to sell the store." Either that or shut it down. But hopefully it wouldn't come to that. Closing the store felt like erasing part of his dad's memory.

"That's a shame. You'd be perfect. You've got a sharp mind, and you're good with people. You could really make it a success."

Maybe he could, but staying in central Florida was out of the question. There were too many memories, too much water under the bridge.

"I guess you know Melissa's staying at the Tyler place." She tilted her head toward the end of the street.

"I knew she was back," he answered, with the eerie sense that she had read his mind. "I just didn't know where."

Marge nodded. When everything blew up between him and Melissa, Marge stayed neutral. Most of the other townspeople didn't. News spread, and his status plummeted overnight from favored fiancé to rotten scumbag.

She flashed him a sympathetic smile. "I thought you should know."

"Thanks," he responded, returning her smile. But it really didn't matter. He wasn't staying in Florida long enough for it to become a problem.

"And thank *you*. I'll see you Saturday."

So Melissa was staying at the Tyler place. He followed the circle drive and braked to a stop at the road. One quick glance to check for traffic. That was all he would allow himself. But his eyes refused to obey. They traveled to the end of Shadowood, past the place where asphalt disappeared and trees swallowed the Tylers' gravel drive.

Red-and-blue lights flashed through the greenery. Adrenaline spiked through him, and he forced himself to pause and think. She had help. Whatever had happened, Harmony Grove police would see to her safety.

But were they prepared? Did they even know the dangers she faced?

He hesitated a moment longer, then raced down the street. He was a public servant, sworn to defend and protect. And he couldn't forget that oath simply because he'd left Memphis.

He ground to a halt behind the cruiser parked in the driveway. Just as he stepped from his truck, Melissa followed a uniformed officer out the front door. The tension contracting his muscles fled so rapidly that a wave of weakness flooded him.

He summoned a professional tone. "Everything all right?"

"Everything's fine." It was the officer who answered, a man he now recognized.

"Alan, hi. This is a surprise. When did you get into law enforcement?"

"I just finished the police academy in June."

"Congratulations. So what happened here?" Nothing against Alan, but three months' experience wasn't exactly reassuring.

"Everything's fine." Melissa repeated Alan's words. "I had a broken window, so I called the cops. Better to be safe than sorry."

"And?"

"It was nothing," she said. "Just a tree branch."

He turned to Alan. "Did you take prints around the window?"

"Uh, no, I didn't."

Melissa cut in. "It wasn't necessary. Tree branches don't leave prints."

He ignored the annoyance in her voice. "Let me see how the branch landed."

"Um, it's not there." Alan shifted his weight from one foot to the other. "I moved it."

"Did you take pictures before you moved it?" His words came out sharper than he intended. But she didn't need her safety further jeopardized by shoddy police work.

"No, I—I didn't think about it."

Melissa put both hands on her hips. "It's okay. We did a nice chalk outline before we moved it." Sarcasm dripped from her tone. "Look, Chris, this isn't your jurisdiction. It's Alan's. So butt out."

Alan cleared his throat and once again shifted his weight. "I better get back to the station."

Chris watched him walk to the patrol car, a pang of guilt stabbing him. He'd been a little hard on the kid. But he needed to learn—a good detective doesn't discount anything, no matter how insignificant. Of course, if Alan didn't know Melissa's history, the situation wouldn't trigger any alarms, especially in a sleepy town like Harmony Grove. From Alan's view, the investigation was simple—branch down, window broken, nothing else disturbed. Act of God. Case closed.

And knowing Melissa, Alan had none of her history. She always was stubborn and independent.

She turned flashing blue eyes on him. "That was uncalled for."

"What?"

"Making Alan feel incompetent."

"I wasn't trying to make him feel incompetent. He just wasn't thorough enough."

"Under the circumstances, he was plenty thorough enough. A limb blew down. It's not a murder investigation."

"Tell me why you left Atlanta."

Something flashed across her features, so briefly

he might have imagined it. Then the mask of indifference snapped back into place. "I already told you. I came here to house sit for the Tylers."

"Melissa, you're running from something. Tell me what it is so I can help."

"Do I look like I'm running?" She crossed her arms in front of her, defiant pose and firmly set jaw daring him to argue.

He expelled a frustrated sigh. Stubborn to a fault. "Are you sure no one went into your house?"

"I'm positive. Alan and I searched every room, and nothing has been touched."

"What about the broken window? Your house isn't very secure right now."

"I've got it under control."

Her tone was growing more and more clipped. But he couldn't walk away knowing the house wasn't secure. "Let me board it up for you."

"I appreciate your concern, but I'm perfectly capable of taking care of myself."

He studied her for several moments, then turned and strode back to his truck. "I've never doubted that for one second."

She was capable, all right. Capable, independent, intelligent and exasperatingly stubborn. And something told him she was in over her head.

Maybe there was a reason their paths had crossed. Not anything so grand as divine intervention. More like fate. God had a universe to run. He was too busy to get involved in the details. It was up to man to make his destiny.

But first he had to know what he was up against. And that wouldn't happen until he heard from Ron.

Which had better be soon.

Or one off-duty Memphis detective was going to lose his mind.

# THREE

"You seem distracted. What's up?"

Melissa eyed BethAnn Benson across the large pepperoni-and-mushroom pizza on the table between them. It wouldn't do any good to deny it. BethAnn knew her too well. All through grade school and middle school, they were inseparable—her, Beth-Ann and Adrianne—until BethAnn's father landed a job in Orlando. Then it was just her and Adrianne.

"I got flowers." It wasn't Valentine's Day, her birthday was two months ago and no congratulations were in order. But when she got home that afternoon, a dozen red roses waited on her front porch.

BethAnn's brows rose. "That's a bad thing?"

"They were left anonymously."

BethAnn pursed her lips, concern etched into her features. "Knowing your history, that's just creepy. Any chance they could be from Eugene?"

"I thought of that. But it doesn't seem like something he would do. Maybe early on." Back then, he was just a friendly neighbor who shared her laundry night and occasionally talked her into walking across the street for ice cream. There wasn't even anything scary about him. Maybe a little quirky, like how he always carried a notebook but would never show her what was inside, and how he entertained her with more tales of adventure than could ever happen in a single lifetime. She didn't even try to separate fact from fiction. But with his buzz cut, muscled arms and tough-guy tattoo, the war stories probably had some root in reality.

"We moved beyond the possibility of flowers the first time he pinned me against the fitness room wall with his hand around my throat." A shudder shook her shoulders. Things went from interesting to scary overnight. Laundry, working out, visiting the pool—wherever she went, he was never far behind. Soon he began to threaten any man that looked her way. Once she got the restraining order, those threats were turned on her.

No, if Eugene ever found her, the last thing he would do was bring her flowers. Unless he was de-mented enough to think he had a chance of wooing her. If so, he wasn't just scary; he was insane.

"At any rate," she continued, "I don't think he could have found me. He doesn't have my new name. There's nothing connecting me to the house. And I never told him where I'm from." Even when he said that as a child he spent a summer with his cousins in Fort Meade, she hadn't revealed her roots—Fort Meade was too close to Harmony Grove.

"Maybe the flowers are from Chris." BethAnn's

green eyes sparked with mischief, and her blond curls bobbed with each movement of her head. If there was one word to describe BethAnn, it was *enthusiastic,* a quality that was especially present when the topic was romance.

Melissa looked at her askance. "Why would Chris send me flowers?"

"I don't know. To butter you up? To make amends for past wrongs?"

"He thought he was justified, remember?"

BethAnn shrugged. "Have you seen him this week?"

"He was at the house yesterday, throwing his weight around and telling Alan how to do his job."

BethAnn's brow creased. "What was Alan doing at your place?"

"I had a broken window. Turns out it was just a tree limb."

"You sure?" The creases were still there.

"You're as bad as Chris. I'm positive." She picked up her fork and pushed a bite-size piece of pizza across her plate. "Anyway, Chris had no business butting in like that."

"He was worried about you. I think that's sweet."

"It's his police training, nothing more, which is fine with me. Believe me, I'm over him."

BethAnn's gaze narrowed. "Then why haven't you dated?"

"I've dated…some." She pushed the piece of pizza back across her plate, her tone a little defensive.

"Who?"

"Pete, for one, the guy I met at the gym."

"You were just friends. You told me so yourself. So Pete doesn't count. Who else?"

Great. BethAnn wanted real dates. Okay, she had a few of those, too, complete with flowers. "Keith."

"Three dates is too brief to count."

Then that would eliminate Dan and Richard, too.

"Who have you dated *seriously?* If it wasn't for those weekly calls and emails for the past five years, maybe you could fool me."

"I was too busy to get serious with anyone. The first three years I was putting myself through school. And the last four months I've been here."

"Well, Chris wasn't any angel," BethAnn began, "but I blame Adrianne more than him."

"Maybe so. But when I walked into his apartment that night, he wasn't exactly putting up a fight. They were wrapped so tightly in each other's arms, a paper clip wouldn't fit between them." She expelled a disgusted sigh. "Here I was, crazy in love, three weeks before my wedding, and there was my fiancé in the arms of my best friend."

Blackness settled over her soul, followed by an immediate prick of conviction. She had felt quite a few of those lately. And Sunday's sermon didn't help, something about leaving your gift at the altar and making things right with the one who wronged you. But how could she forgive someone who completely knocked her world off its axis?

Of course, that was *her* fault. She should have known better. Her father had taught her well—men are faithful until something better comes along. He walked out, straight into the arms of another woman, her mother fell apart, and suddenly the nine-year-old child became the responsible adult.

She stabbed the bite of pizza that had traveled around her plate for the past several minutes, but couldn't bring it to her mouth. Playing with her food was more appealing than eating it. And it wasn't the fault of the pizza. For thirty years, Pappy's Pizzeria had served the thickest, tastiest pizza south of the Mason-Dixon line. And during that time, nothing had changed—not the cracker decor with its scuffed hardwood floors, not its status as a favorite gathering spot for most of Harmony Grove, and certainly not its sumptuous fare that could compete with any big-city Italian restaurant.

She laid her fork back down. "If finding him with Adrianne wasn't bad enough, he really sealed it with that Lance comment."

That was another memory permanently etched in her brain—Chris staring at her, eyes pained and haunted, and making that ridiculous accusation: *I know about Lance.* "Lance was nothing but a brief mistake. Long before I met Chris, I figured out Lance's greatest love was himself. But Chris was convinced I was fooling around with him."

BethAnn shook her head. "Chris didn't seem like the jealous type."

"He wasn't normally. Just with Lance. About a year after I graduated, Lance started trying to get me back. I was dating Chris by then and wasn't interested. But Chris still felt threatened."

BethAnn laid down the slice of pizza she held and wiped her hand on the paper napkin in her lap. *Her* appetite was obviously still intact. She was currently polishing off her third slice. "You know, Adrianne always was jealous of you."

"Jealous of *me?*" She eyed BethAnn with raised brows. "How? *She* was the one who got anything she wanted."

"You got the good grades without even trying. Everybody liked you, your dry wit, your sarcastic sense of humor. And you had Chris. She never came out and said it, but I could read between the lines." BethAnn had come back for regular weekend visits, so she had kept in contact with Adrianne, too. "But I have to admit, this totally caught me off guard."

"You and me both. I knew she was a flirt, but I somehow thought *my* man would be off-limits. Pretty naive, I guess."

BethAnn stared into the distance and worked her wedding band around her finger with her thumb. "You know, you were both pretty young then."

"He was twenty-four, I was twenty. What are you getting at?"

BethAnn shrugged. "Oh, I don't know. Maybe he turned to Adrianne on impulse, and he's learned his lesson."

Melissa gave her a wry smile. If anyone saw the world through rose-colored glasses, it was Beth-Ann. But there was no sugarcoating what Chris did. "Three months is hardly on impulse."

"Did Chris tell you it had been going on for three months?"

"No, Adrianne did."

"And you believed her?"

"Why not? I mean, Chris didn't jump in with any defense. Just his stupid accusations about Lance."

"Well, he still cares about you, or he wouldn't have been over there giving Alan a hard time. You ought to just call him and ask about the flowers."

"I don't have his number."

"Jamison Marine. I'm sure it's in the phone book. If he admits to leaving the flowers, you can stop worrying about Eugene."

"You've got a point."

Except it would take a lot more than a call to Chris to stop worrying about Eugene.

"Since when do we put dock lines with fishing tackle?"

Chris's hand stopped midair as he looked at Derrick, his assistant manager. He didn't have a good answer. Three weeks ago, he could have claimed ignorance. By now he knew his way around his father's marine store so well he could draw it in his sleep.

"Good question. Preoccupied, I guess." He carried

the packages to the end of the rack and hung them from a metal peg.

"I bet it's a woman."

Chris snickered. "Just because you're madly in love doesn't mean everyone else has lost touch with reality."

A goofy grin took over Derrick's face. A week and a half from his wedding date, he had some concentration issues of his own.

But Derrick's assessment was dead-on. It was a woman, all right. A woman with delicate features and haunted eyes. A woman who was afraid and trying her hardest not to show it. Five days had passed since he'd talked to Ron, and he still didn't know anything. His anxiety was growing with each passing hour.

Monday's broken window didn't help. Melissa was satisfied with the branch explanation. He couldn't brush it off so easily. Just because nothing was taken didn't mean someone hadn't gone inside. But without prints, there was no way of knowing.

For the eighty-ninth time that day, he pushed her from his mind and dragged his thoughts back to his work. The cardboard box he had been unpacking was now empty—Derrick removed the last three items some time ago. He picked up the box and, on his way to the back of the store, stopped at one of the two offices behind the counter. "How are you coming with the books?"

"Just about there," Donna answered without looking up. Stacks of checks and different denominations of bills dotted her desk. "I'll be ready to run financial statements shortly."

It was about time. He couldn't believe it when he took over the store and found dozens of handwritten ledgers. His father was in the Dark Ages. So was his bookkeeper. How was he supposed to sell the store with no legitimate financial statements?

"Great. I'd like to sit down with you Friday and go over what you have." A deadline wouldn't hurt, given her history. He'd purchased a user-friendly accounting program and had been prodding her since day one to get the bookkeeping computerized.

Donna looked up from the deposit slip she was filling out but didn't make eye contact. "Anything in particular you're looking for?"

"Let's start with balance sheets, operating statements and bank reconciliations for the first quarter. Then we'll go from there."

"I'll do my best." She sat straight and stiff, as if ready to bolt at any moment.

"Donna?"

Her eyes darted away the instant they met his.

"Relax. It's not an IRS audit. It's not even a performance review."

All he got for his efforts was a tentative smile.

She was such a mousy woman. Accountant types weren't the life of the party, but Donna made keeping to herself an art form. He had worked with her three days a week for the past few weeks, and all he knew was that she was thirty-five, married, lived in

Winter Haven and was a U.S. citizen. And that much he owed to her W-4 and I-9. But she apparently knew her stuff. For over eight years, his father had trusted her totally.

At the thought of his father, grief pressed down on him. If only he'd known his dad's time was so short. He would have come back more often. Or maybe he would have never left.

He trudged to the office next door and sank into the worn-out swivel chair that sat behind an equally well-used desk. His dad's office. What was supposed to eventually be his own.

When he decided to go into police work instead of taking over the store, his father had understood. But his leaving Florida had been hard on the old man. They had always been close. Ever since he was six years old and his mother decided she couldn't cope with the responsibility of a husband and child, it had been just the two of them.

He never saw his mother again. At the time, he was too young to understand. In fact, he still didn't. She should have loved him enough to hang in there. Instead, she calmly extricated herself from the little body entwined around her legs, strode quickly to her car and drove away. And that was that.

His cell phone rang, and when he glanced at the number on the screen, energy surged through him. He had waited five days for this call. "Hey, Ron. Have you got something for me?"

"Sorry it took me a while to get back to you." His partner's bass voice boomed through the phone. "It looks like your lady filed a restraining order against a Eugene Holmes for stalking. Seems he took quite an unhealthy liking to her and wouldn't leave her alone. So she got the restraining order. That's when things got scary. He's one of those if-I-can't-have-her-nobody-can guys. There are several police reports. The last one she filed, the perp had a knife to her throat, when someone walked up, and he took off. He's apparently pretty slick, because they've never caught him."

As Ron talked, dread trickled over him. He knew the type. Some guys just didn't give up until they were behind bars. If everyone was lucky, that happened before anyone got hurt. Too often it didn't.

He rubbed his eyelids with a thumb and index finger, then put his head in his hand. This was what he was afraid of. "Well, thanks for checking it out."

At least now he had an idea of what he was up against. He shook his head. No, *he* wasn't up against anything. Protecting her wasn't his responsibility. She was a citizen of Harmony Grove. That's what the Harmony Grove Police Department was there for—to protect its citizens. Let them see to her safety.

Somehow that wasn't very reassuring. Alan was a nice enough guy and probably took his job seriously. But he was so green, he blended with the shrubbery. Then there was Chief Branch, with boatloads more experience but a fraction of the concern, especially when Melissa was involved. Unless things had changed in the past five years, Branch had it in for both Langston women, over some perceived wrong that nobody quite understood.

"There's a call for you on line one," Derrick announced from the front counter. "A Melissa Morris."

Melissa? What would she be calling about? He walked up front and put the phone to his ear.

"This is going to sound pretty off-the-wall," she began, "but…you didn't send me flowers, did you?"

For several moments, he sat in dumb silence, feeling like someone who had walked into the middle of a movie and missed all the important scenes. "What?"

"Flowers showed up on my doorstep yesterday afternoon. You didn't send them, did you?"

"No, I didn't." Uneasiness nibbled at the edges of his mind. Flowers were hardly a threatening gesture. But for a woman in Melissa's position, everything took on grave meaning. "Was there a card?"

"It said, 'Just to let you know I'm thinking about you.' No signature or anything." She paused and gave a short laugh, but there was no humor in the sound. "I guess I have a secret admirer."

"Have you checked with Flanagan Florist? If they came from there, Sandy could probably tell you who ordered them." He wanted to warn her of the danger she was in. But if she knew he had used his connections to check on her, she would be furious. Judging from the tension in her tone and the apprehension that seemed to always cling to her, though, the warnings were probably unnecessary.

"Sandy's cards say 'Flanagan Florist.' This one doesn't."

He picked up a pen and began to tap it against the wood surface of the desk. Harmony Grove P.D. needed to have the history Ron had just given him. But knowing Melissa, she hadn't told them a thing. If he could just get her to talk… "You sound like this is really bugging you, more than just curiosity."

"You know me—can't stand an unsolved mystery." She forced another one of those uncomfortable laughs.

"Well, frankly, it's bugging me. The whole situation makes me uneasy. I'm going to give you my cell number, and I want you to program it into your phone."

"I'm fine, really. I don't need—"

"Just humor me. Please?"

A heavy sigh came through the phone. "All right. What is it?"

He gave her the number. "Now program it in and call me back."

"I'll do it later. Look, everything's fine. I don't need your help."

"I know you don't. You can handle everything on your own." He tried to keep the sarcasm from his tone but wasn't quite successful. Her stubbornness was downright exasperating. "You're humoring me, remember? Just go ahead and program it and call me back."

"When did you turn into such a worrywart?" She cut the connection without waiting for an answer. Two minutes later she dialed him back. "You happy now?"

"I'll sleep like a baby tonight."

She had his number, and it was easily accessible. Now it was time to pay Alan a visit.


Something awoke her.

Melissa pulled the comforter to her chin and lay stock-still in the darkness, listening. Waiting.

A series of dull flickers filled the room. The muted rumble didn't come until almost a half minute later. The storm couldn't be what woke her up. It was too far away. The thunder was so faint, she had to be listening for it to even notice, and the light passing through the sheers didn't provide much more illumination than the total darkness it briefly replaced.

The rumble faded to silence, and uneasiness enveloped her. Every sense shot to full alert. Something wasn't right. She could feel it.

A distinct creak shattered the silence, and a chill passed over her. After more than four months, she should be used to the sounds of the old wood-frame house. But each creak and groan sent apprehension spiraling through her. Especially in the middle of the night.

She clutched the comforter more tightly and listened. A gust of wind swept through, a precursor to the storm, and a low-hanging branch scraped the roof. Maybe that was what had awoken her. She would see about having someone trim the branches away from the house. That was one bump in the night she could control.

Another creak sounded, sending icy tendrils of fear slithering up her spine. She recognized that creak. It was the same sound a few of the steps made under her weight.

Was someone in the house?

For several moments, she lay paralyzed, ears cocked and eyes riveted on the open door. But the only sound besides the howling of the wind was her own pounding heart. And she couldn't see anything in the near blackness.

Lightning flashed in the distance, casting its eerie pulsating glow.

And a fresh wave of terror crashed down on her.

Someone stood in the open doorway of her room.

# FOUR

A bloodcurdling scream was wrenched from her throat, and panic careened through her body. Frantic prayers circled her mind, chopped pleas for help.

Where was he? Had her scream scared him away? Or was he in the room with her?

Another series of flashes sifted through the sheer panels. Her gaze darted a jagged path around the room. She was alone. Even the doorway was empty. She thrust the comforter aside and sprinted for the door, slamming it shut and turning the lock in one swift motion.

For several moments, she stood frozen. Her mind screamed unintelligible commands, and her heart hammered against her rib cage. She needed to do something.

Call someone. BethAnn. No, she could get hurt. Chris. His number would be at the top of her recent calls.

She snatched her phone from the nightstand and flipped it open. The first beep sounded amplified, even against the backdrop of the storm building outside. Another bolt of panic shot through her. *Lord, please help me.* If her intruder knew she was calling for help, he might break down the door.

She took a steadying breath. God could protect her. She knew that. Was it showing a lack of faith to wish for more? If only she had a weapon—a bat, a knife, anything. But a mental inventory of her closet produced nothing more intimidating than some high-heeled shoes and her scantily stocked purse. She pressed the call key once more and stood straight and stiff, eyes riveted on the locked door, praying with all her might that it stay closed and wondering what she would do if it didn't.

One ring sounded, and she snapped her phone shut. What was she doing? She needed to call the police. They would be there in minutes and were armed and trained to handle her prowler. Chris was, too—trained at least, and probably even armed. But she didn't want his help.

She dialed nine-one-one, put in her request and disconnected the call, heart still pounding out its erratic rhythm. When the phone suddenly began to vibrate, it almost fell from her hand. She jerked it open before the ringtone could begin.

"Melissa, did you try to call?"

She groaned inwardly. *No, not Chris.* His phone couldn't have rung for more than a second or two. But even as she groused, she couldn't deny the sense of relief that tumbled through her the instant she heard his voice. "I changed my mind," she whispered. "Sorry I disturbed you."

"Okay. Tell me what's going on. And this time you're not brushing me off."

She closed her eyes and drew in a slow, deep breath. She shouldn't tell him. If he thought she was in danger, he would never leave her alone.

But the words spilled out anyway.

"Someone's in my house."

An audible "umph" announced Chris's springing from his bed. "Lock your bedroom door and call the police."

Funny, he figured out in five seconds what took her five minutes. Of course, he wasn't scared out of his mind. "I already have."

"Then stay put. I'll be right there. And I'm not hanging up."

The wind picked up, releasing its rage in intermittent howls. Soon rain began to pelt the windows. She sat back on the bed and pulled the comforter around her, suddenly chilled. In fact, she couldn't stop shivering.

"Are you still with me?" The scrape of opening and closing drawers punctuated his words.

"I'm here," she whispered, willing him to hurry. Moments later, flashing lights turned the lacy curtains red-and-blue, and relief washed over her. "The police are here."

"Don't hang up until you let them inside."

That sense of security fled almost immediately.

She had to make it to the front door. For several moments she stood, phone pressed to her ear and her other hand resting on the bedroom doorknob. Where was her intruder?

A heavy knock reverberated through the house. If she didn't get downstairs soon, the police would kick their way in. With her pulse pounding in her ears, she unlocked the bedroom door and slowly pulled it open. The hinges responded with a protesting squeak. Another flash offered brief illumination, then once again plunged everything into blackness. If she could just get to the front door...

The hallway was still, the other bedrooms shadowed caverns, dark and ominous. She forced herself to tiptoe from the relative safety of her room, then, stealth forgotten, broke into a full sprint, panic snapping at her heels. Her bare feet slapped the hardwood floor and pounded down the steps, skidding to a stop at the front door. The *locked* front door. Brow creased, she looked through the peephole, then released the dead bolt.

Chief Branch stood on the porch wearing a dripping yellow rain slicker and an irritated scowl. What was *he* doing responding to a call in the middle of the night? He always left that to one of his subordinates. He lifted a bored gaze to hers and shook his head. "Less than five months back in Harmony Grove and you're already being a problem."

Her panic of several moments ago was swept aside by annoyance. She would have laughed off a comment like that from anyone else. But Branch wasn't joking. For as long as she could remember, their relationship had been one of tolerance, with the occasional jab thrown in for good measure. "I figured you'd send Alan or Tommy rather than lose any of your beauty sleep."

"Tommy's on vacation, and Alan spent all day with his grandmother at Lakeland Regional. I told him I'd cover tonight." He spoke with a heavy Southern drawl, a typical small-town cop, but without the friendliness. "So what seems to be the problem?"

"I woke up, and a man was standing in my bedroom doorway." He raised both brows but didn't comment, so she continued. "I screamed, and he disappeared. I guess I scared him away."

"Well, let me have a look inside, and I'll see if I can figure out how he got in."

Watching him pocket his flashlight and hang his rain jacket on the hall tree, she wished it was Alan or Tommy who'd responded. Branch never liked her, and she had no idea why. She had never had any brushes with the law, not even a speeding ticket.

Whatever his reasons, she wasn't too crazy about him, either. He always walked with the swagger of someone who thought way too much of himself. Granted, he was chief. But chief of two hardly qualified him for national recognition.

He walked into the living room, where he began to separate slats in the blinds, checking the window latches behind them. "Everything was locked when you went to bed?"

"Definitely." After five years in the city, that was a given. Even more so since encountering Eugene.

"What about the front door? Before you opened it just now, was it locked?"

"It was."

He went through each room checking the locks, searching for signs of forced entry. The effort earned him some labored breathing, accompanied by a slight wheeze. The dark blue uniform stretched taut over his substantial paunch, threatening to send a button sailing through the air, and the black leather belt holding his holster looked painfully tight. He obviously spent more time sitting behind a desk than apprehending criminals.

She followed him into the kitchen, where he crossed the room to check the back door. It was locked, too. The same held true for the kitchen window. He nodded toward the end of the short hall that separated the pantry from the broom closet. "Does that door go to the garage?"

"Yes, it does." At least it used to be a garage. The Tylers had traded the garage door for a sliding glass door, with plans to turn the space into a game room and build a carport off the back. But that was as far as they had gotten. So she was left with a monster-size laundry room and lots of storage space. And two choices for entry—a trek up the sidewalk to the front door or a hike around back.

Chief Branch reappeared within moments. "Well, I've checked the entire downstairs, and there's no sign of forced entry anywhere. Does anyone have a key besides you?"

"Just the Tylers and Mrs. Johnson next door. I know it wasn't Mrs. Johnson, and the Tylers are in Washington."

"Well, I think it's safe to assume no one could get in from the second floor. So either you didn't see what you thought you saw or you were dreaming."

A wave of uneasiness swept over her. She wasn't dreaming—someone had stood in her doorway. She was sure of it. And she wouldn't be convinced otherwise until every square inch of the house had been searched. "Would you please check upstairs anyway?"

He didn't respond, just gave her that expression of condescension that he had perfected so well.

"I wasn't dreaming," she insisted. "I was fully awake and had been for several minutes. I know what I saw."

Branch shrugged. "No problem. I'll search upstairs, too. Your intruder might have had an extension ladder…or a bucket truck. We've had a lot of those cases lately."

Annoyance surged up again, but before she could respond, the front door swung open and a panicked male voice called her name. Chris stood in the foyer, hovering at the threshold, creases of worry lining his face. The creases smoothed and disappeared the instant he saw her.

Suddenly she was in his arms and wasn't even sure how she got there. Relief washed over her, sweeping away the uneasiness that clung to her even after Branch's arrival. She pressed her cheek against his chest and drew in his masculine scent, fresh as a mountain stream, mixed with a hint of the woods. It was a scent that bespoke strength and safety and dependability.

Then something stirred deep inside, a whispered warning. Nagging doubts clawed their way to the surface. It didn't matter how safe she felt in his arms. She was clinging to a mirage, a sweet-smelling vapor that would, without a moment's notice, disappear into the mist.

She would never be able to trust him with her heart.

If she thought otherwise, she was a fool.

Suddenly Melissa stiffened and pulled from his embrace. "I'm sorry. I was just— I shouldn't have done that."

As he watched her turn and walk away, acute emptiness wrapped around his soul. For one exquisite moment, he held her tightly against him, his face buried in that luxurious mane of hair. The years that separated them melted away, along with everything ugly that had ever come between them.

Then just as quickly, the moment was gone and he was alone, arms cold and empty.

He caught up to her in the living room. She stood

with her back to him, hair falling in disarray about her shoulders, silk robe fluttering with each breath. She looked so beautiful. And so…vulnerable. It was all he could do to stay where he was and not haul her back into his arms.

He cleared his throat, and she turned to face him, stiff and uncomfortable.

And he wasn't so comfortable himself. He had no business feeling the way he did. Wanting to protect her was okay. It was his job. Maybe not in Harmony Grove, but that was what he did—protect the public. And that was what he would do for Melissa. Anything more would be out of line.

He hauled in a deep breath. "Look, don't feel bad about what happened out there. It was a natural reaction—relief and gratitude at seeing a friendly face. And I didn't take it as anything more."

The corners of her mouth quivered upward. "Thanks."

He tried for some levity, for his own sake as much as hers. "Next time you need a friendly hug, keep me in mind. I'm always ready to lend a helping hand."

She smiled more broadly. "Thanks. I'll remember that."

He needed to change the subject, because all he could think about was how warm and soft she had felt in his arms. "Have they found anything? Any sign of forced entry?"

"Nothing downstairs. He's checking upstairs now."

Concern crept across her features, darkening those crystal-blue eyes.

Heavy tread sounded on the stairs, and moments later, Chief Branch strolled into the living room. The years hadn't been as kind to him as they had to Melissa. Hair that was thinning five years earlier had vacated completely, leaving behind a pale, shiny scalp. His trek down the stairs had left him gasping for air, and the massive belly announced just how out of shape he had become, a warning poster for what can happen with too many donuts and too little exercise.

If the old chief was surprised to see him, he didn't show it. He just gave a brief nod and turned to Melissa. "Nothing upstairs, either. The entire house is locked up tight. There's no need to dust for prints."

"I don't understand. I could have sworn…" Her voice trailed off, worry etching itself more deeply into her features.

"It was dark. Your eyes were playing tricks on you."

While the chief strolled to his patrol car, Chris waited with her in the foyer. With a heavy sigh, she sank back against an oak chest that sat along one wall and closed her eyes. "I feel like an idiot. But it seemed so real."

Her dejected pose stirred something in him that went far beyond mere civic duty. He didn't want to just see to her safety—he wanted to draw her into his arms and hold her until all the tension fled her body. He curbed the desire and settled instead for a reassuring hand on her shoulder. "Tell me about it."

She drew in a shaky breath, eyes twin pools of concern. "The storm was coming, but I don't think that's what woke me. I heard creaks, you know, like old houses make. But this sounded like someone was coming up the stairs. Then there was a flash of lightning, and I saw someone standing in the doorway. At least I thought I did. I guess I heard the creaks and let my imagination run away with me." She attempted a small smile but wasn't quite successful.

Suddenly her brow creased. "I just realized something. I haven't seen my cat."

"He's probably sleeping somewhere."

"No, he always sleeps with me."

He followed her up the stairs toward what he guessed was her bedroom. When she dropped to her hands and knees beside the bed, he circled around to the other side and lifted the bed skirt. Wide gold eyes peered out from a solid white face.

"Well, hello, kitty. What are you doing hiding under there?"

The cat hissed and took a swipe at him. He jerked his hand back. "Whoa, I just about got zapped."

In three seconds flat, Melissa was beside him. "He never hisses."

She pulled him from his hiding place and rose to her feet, holding him against her chest. The contented rumble began almost immediately. "Meet Smudge."

He scratched the top of the cat's head and moved to

the furry cheeks. The purring grew louder. "I didn't know you were a cat person."

"I wasn't, but Smudge changed that. He showed up at my apartment cold, starving and soaking wet. And when I discovered he was deaf, that clinched it. I had to keep him." She laid the cat on the bed and stroked his back a couple more times. "He's usually really friendly. Something must have scared him."

"Maybe it was having Chief Branch in here tromping through your house. You know, really big, strange guy in a uniform."

He stepped back and let his gaze scan the room. A mahogany four-poster bed occupied one wall, with a coordinating dresser and chest of drawers on two others. In the corner, a water pitcher and bowl sat atop an antique stand.

"This is a really nice place."

"I know. It's like getting to live in my dream house. It's even furnished the way I like."

He raised his brows. "It is? When did you get interested in antiques?"

"A couple of years ago. A friend in Atlanta was looking for some antique china to replace missing pieces in her great-grandmother's set. While she checked out dishes, I browsed the furniture, and it really started to grow on me. My apartment was furnished, but I picked up a few smaller pieces here and there." She pointed to the corner. "The water pitcher and stand are mine. So is the Bombay chest in the foyer."

"So you now like cats *and* antiques."

"And gardening," she added. "I've got a killer garden going right now."

"Any other surprises? You're not getting ready to go Goth or anything, are you?"

A smile lit her eyes. "I might have some other surprises, but that won't be one of them. I don't look good in black."

She made two more strokes down the cat's back and walked from the room. "I'm sorry I bothered you. I panicked and called you before I thought it through." She turned at the top of the stairs and gave him a weak smile.

"Don't worry about it. That's why I gave you my number. I'd much rather get a false alarm than find out you were in danger and didn't call."

He followed her down the steps and into the foyer, where she turned to face him.

"Are you going to be okay alone? I can crash the rest of the night on the living room couch if you'd like."

"No, I'll be fine." She reached out and brushed her fingers against his arm, her touch featherlight. "Thanks for rushing over here. That was sweet."

He nodded slowly, feeling the tug of everything that had drawn him to her all those years ago, mixed with a solid dose of regret. If only he hadn't listened to Adrianne. But she had been so convincing, dropping hints, then making him pry it out of her. And the confession had left him reeling. He had accepted her comforting hug. But when she had locked him in a sudden kiss, he had been too stunned to react. That was the moment Melissa had walked in. And all he'd done was hurl accusations.

"I'm sorry," he whispered. "For everything."

Her eyes glistened with unshed tears, but she blinked them away before they could pool against her lower lashes. "Don't worry about it. It's all in the past. What's done is done, and we can't go back and change it…even if we wanted to." Something in her tone said she didn't.

At one time, they'd had something special. At least he thought they had. But she walked away so easily. She didn't even care enough to work through it, to try to reassure him that what Adrianne said was a lie. She'd just left. And it almost destroyed him.

But why should he have expected anything different? How could he trust her to stay when his own mother hadn't? If there was one thing life had taught him, it was not to count on any kind of long-term commitment. Because no matter how perfect everything seemed, eventually that all-important person in his life would leave, and he would be right back where he started.

Alone.

# FIVE

Melissa placed the last jewelry kit in the box and smiled at BethAnn. "That's all of it. And there are more empty boxes than full ones, so that's a good sign."

The park had been a flurry of activity all day. Once again, the Harmony Grove Fall Festival and Craft Fair was a smashing success. Now, at five o'clock, the visitors had gone, and everyone left was boxing merchandise, disassembling canopies and cleaning up any trash left behind.

BethAnn took the box and stacked it on the hand truck with the other two. "I'm pooped. I bet we got thirty people signed up for my workshops, and I don't even know how many craft kits we sold. Thanks for your help. I couldn't have handled it by myself."

"No problem. I enjoyed it." The only downside was being in such close proximity to Chris all day. She couldn't believe it when he showed up shortly after she arrived and began helping Marge Tandy set up a booth catty-corner from BethAnn's. Fortunately, there hadn't been enough lulls during the day to pay much attention to what he was doing a few yards away.

BethAnn started to pull the tablecloth from the table. "Everyone says last year was the best fair ever, but I think we had an even bigger turnout this year."

Melissa reached for the other end of the tablecloth. She couldn't vouch for last year's turnout, but it had been a long time since she had seen so many people in one spot. All day long, moving from one booth to the next had involved navigating through a maze of bodies. The vendors, half of whom were from outside Harmony Grove, offered everything from paintings to hand-carved wood to stained glass and pottery. And the groups performing at thirty-minute intervals on the center stage were just as varied. As always, the contest tent was a popular spot, with the gaudy four-inch "Harmony Grove Champ" medallion as the prize for every victory, whether raising the biggest eggplant or eating the most pancakes.

Melissa tried unsuccessfully to stifle a yawn. "As much as I enjoyed it, I'm glad it's over. I went to sleep way too late and then was up at four baking eight dozen cookies."

BethAnn grinned over at her. "Nothing like waiting till the last minute."

"I know. But they're so much better fresh." She looked past BethAnn to see Chris remove a painting from its easel and stand it on a cart with several others. In his boat shoes, cargo shorts, sailfish-print shirt and bucket cap, he looked like he was ready for a day on one of his dad's boats.

BethAnn followed her gaze. "I think you should give it another try."

"Out of the question. I'd never be able to trust him. Besides, he doesn't want a relationship. He just wants to get everything wrapped up and get back to his life in Memphis. He told me so."

"Plans can change."

"Not these plans."

Chris looked up suddenly and waved a greeting, one which was returned enthusiastically by BethAnn. "Don't you think it's odd your paths have crossed after all these years?"

"Not really. I mean, this *is* where we're both from."

"But you both left and were never going to come back. What if God is trying to bring you back together? He *does* work in mysterious ways."

*There she goes, bringing God into it.* But that was expected. BethAnn found the Lord right before returning to Harmony Grove, and her faith colored everything she did. In fact, it was her testimony that had led Melissa to make her own commitment.

BethAnn grasped the hand truck and began rolling it toward the sidewalk. "So why did you get to sleep so late?"

Melissa shrugged. "Just tense, I guess. Still on edge from my scare a couple nights ago. When it's late and I'm all alone in that big old house, it gets kind of spooky." That was part of it, anyway. Wednesday night's scare had shaken her in an entirely different way. Having Chris rush over, seeing the concern on that handsome face, feeling the strength and protection of those muscular arms, and knowing that, at least for a few fleeting moments, she didn't have to face it alone—the whole experience had left her yearning for something she didn't even realize she needed.

And last night was the worst. She tossed and turned till midnight, then opted for some chamomile tea and a novel. Two cups and forty pages later, exhaustion kicked in, and she fell into a fitful sleep. But it was much too short. Now she was feeling it.

She slid the last box into the back of BethAnn's van and slammed the door. A Cadillac Escalade crept past, Marge Tandy at the wheel. Chris sat in the passenger's seat. In another twenty minutes, he would have Marge's things unloaded and be headed home. His temporary home, anyway. She turned her gaze back to BethAnn. "Just the table and canopy, and we're done."

"Don't worry about the canopy. Kevin can get it. That's what husbands are for." She shot a glance to the center of the park where a half-dozen men worked to tear down the stage and pack up sound equipment. "Go home and take a nap. You look ready to pass out any second."

She flashed BethAnn a crooked smile. "You won't get any argument from me."

A few minutes later, she pulled into her driveway, that nap forefront in her mind. But halfway up the walk she hesitated. A plain white envelope hung on the front door, her name across the front in bold, black print. As she pulled the tape loose, a chill passed over her, raising the hair on the back of her neck.

The breeze intensified, and she cast a furtive glance over her shoulder. Branches stirred to life, thousands of hushed voices descending on her. She jerked her gaze to the windows. They were still intact. At least the front ones were. And Handy Andy had replaced the shattered glass in back the day after it was broken.

She unlocked the door and stepped into the foyer, pulse pounding in her ears. What was wrong with her? It was just a note, probably left by one of her neighbors. Why did she have to turn it into something ominous?

No amount of silent scolding, however, stilled her racing heart as she tore the seal and pulled the contents from the envelope. It was a single page, thick and unlined, folded in thirds. The print matched that on the envelope. She leaned back against the door and began to read.

*Melissa, my sweetheart. Your beauty surpasses that of the most flawless flower, the finest painting, the grandest sunset. Your perfection is unrivaled.*

*The first moment I laid eyes on you, I knew.*

*From the first lilting words out of your mouth,
my life was changed, and now that I've tasted
the sublime, I will never again be satisfied with
my mundane life.*

She closed her eyes, suddenly feeling dizzy. Was
this a joke? Someone trying to engage in some good-
natured teasing with no idea of her situation? She
tried to steel herself against the nausea churning in
her stomach and returned her gaze to the page.

*But I'm worried about you. Last night your light
was on till 2:30 a.m. You need your sleep. Do
you long for me as I long for you? Soon we'll be
together, and nothing will tear us apart.*

She clamped her hand over her mouth, fighting the
bile rising in her throat. This was no joke. Someone
was watching her. Closely enough that he knew what
time she went to bed the prior night.
*Dear God, please, no, not again.*
She closed her eyes and grasped for a shred of security, some assurance that everything was going
to be okay. There was none. She was standing at the
edge of an abyss, ready to fall in.
And no one was there to catch her.

He shouldn't do it.
He should just leave Harmony Grove and head

back to Lakeland. Melissa didn't want him hovering over her. She had made that clear.

But his conversation with Ron had left him with a bad feeling. It wouldn't go away, no matter how many times he told himself the local police could see to her safety. As long as he was within fifty miles of her, he couldn't resist the need to get involved.

For several moments, he waited at the end of the Tandys' driveway. Then he stepped on the gas and turned right—away from the road leading out of town. All day long, he had been less than thirty feet from her. But other than a quick greeting while they were setting up, and a couple of brief conversations when they each took a break from their assistant vendor positions, they had hardly spoken.

But she never left his thoughts for long. Several times he found himself seeking her out across the crowd, while she made change, bagged purchases and chatted with those who stopped to browse. All the while, she smiled, her tinkling laughter riding to him on the afternoon breeze. But beneath the confident facade was hesitation, the apprehension of someone waiting for the other shoe to drop.

The Melissa of old had always been so self-assured. That Melissa seemed to have vanished, or at least gone into hiding. As he watched her at the park, he saw a vulnerability that wasn't there before. And it was doing funny things to his resolve.

He didn't want to feel anything for her. He needed to keep everything professional—a detective concerned for a woman's safety. She didn't want more than that, anyway. And that was all right. Because who was he to say that she wouldn't do it again? That with the next storm that arose, she wouldn't just walk away? It was a risk he wasn't willing to take.

He shoved the truck into Park and strode up the front walk. When Melissa answered his knock moments later, everything he had tried to squelch while watching her at the park rushed back with a vengeance. Haunted blue eyes stared out from a drawn, pale face, a silent plea floating on the air between them.

"Melissa, what is it? What happened?"

For several moments she stood in silence, her innate self-sufficiency doing battle with the longing, just once, to lean on someone else. At last, the indecision fled her features, and she motioned him inside. He followed her to the living room, where she handed him a sheet of paper, then sank onto the couch. Bold black print filled the page, and as he read, an equally dark cloud settled over his soul.

"Who wrote this?"

"I don't know." She drew in a shaky breath. "It was on my door when I got home from the show."

A sense of protectiveness surged through him. He sat next to her and raised an arm to lightly circle her shoulders. "Does the handwriting look at all familiar?"

"Not really. It's pretty generic—block letters, all caps." She studied the note, lower lip drawn between her teeth. Then the corners of her mouth kicked up in a tentative smile. "The handwriting actually looks a lot like yours."

"Mine and a thousand other guys. We print because we write so poorly."

"Well, I'd say it's safe to eliminate you." She smiled a little more fully, and some of the tension seemed to fall away. Already the color was returning to her face.

He refolded the page, cringing at the thought of how the handling had probably destroyed any prints left behind. "So who do you think wrote this?"

Her gaze drifted away until snagged by some point on the walnut coffee table. "It's probably just a prank by some neighborhood kids."

"Uh-huh." He cast her a doubt-infused glance. It wasn't just her averted eyes. It was her tone, that total lack of conviction. "So what time *did* you go to bed last night?"

She met his eyes, her own filled with resignation. "Two-thirty."

"This isn't a prank, Melissa. Someone's watching you." He waited for a response but didn't get one. "Any ideas? Anyone from your past who might do something like this?" *Talk to me, Missy. I can't help you if you won't talk to me.*

Her gaze returned to that invisible spot on the coffee table. Her hands were clasped together in her lap, clutching one another tightly. As long as he had known her, she had been strong and self-sufficient.

His betrayal, plus five years on her own, evidently hadn't made it any easier to drop the barriers.

She pulled her long, thick braid forward and slid the cloth-covered elastic band from its end. Once she had worked the woven tresses loose, she shook out the dark strands until they flowed in silken waves over her shoulders and down her chest. Did she have any idea what that did to him? Of course she didn't. She was simply doing what she always did—filling uncomfortable moments with activity.

He watched her for some time, silently pleading with her to let him in. Finally she drew in a long, slow breath. "There's only one."

"Who?"

"A guy I knew in Atlanta. He started stalking me. No matter what I did, he wouldn't leave me alone. So I got a restraining order." She continued to stare at the table, her tone flat. "That only made matters worse. By the time the police got there, he was always gone. They were never able to catch him."

"So you changed your name and moved here?"

She nodded slowly and raised her eyes to meet his. Her shoulders rose and fell with each shaky breath, lightly brushing his side. Subtle hints of citrus and spice teased his senses, and the vulnerability on her face shot straight to his heart.

He cleared his throat and corralled his wayward thoughts. He needed to focus on one thing—her safety. "Do the Harmony Grove police know anything about this?"

She shook her head. "Maybe I should tell them."

"There's no maybe to it. You *need* to tell them. And they should know about the flowers and this note. They can drive by here regularly, you know, keep an eye on things."

Her gaze fell back to the table. "I don't think it's him, though."

"Why not?"

She shrugged. "Leaving me flowers and notes just doesn't sound like something he would do. And I don't see how he could have found me. He doesn't have my new name, doesn't know where I went, doesn't know where I'm from and doesn't have the financial means to hire someone to get that information." It was a pep talk aimed at herself as much as him. And judging from the worry lines etched into her features, she wasn't convinced, either.

"I think you should have someone come and stay with you for a while."

"Everybody's got their own lives. I'm not going to impose on anyone like that."

"Look, Melissa, whether it's this guy or not, you've got some nutcase watching you. You shouldn't be alone. How about if I stay? I could sleep on your living room couch."

She shook her head, her tone adamant. "You can't move in here."

"I'll stay in your shed."

"It's a stable," she corrected, "and it's not habitable. The doors don't close properly and it leaks.

The Tylers are planning to have it torn down." That signature independence was back, that stubborn determination that was so characteristic of Melissa. It would be a relief if it weren't for the danger she was in.

"Then let me check on you. And you've got to promise to call at the first sign of danger."

"All right," she agreed, although reluctantly.

"You won't try to play the brave, reckless heroine like you see in the movies?"

Her lips quirked upward. "You mean the kind that hears someone in the house and opens the door to the room with the mysterious light, instead of calling the police?"

"Yeah, that kind."

"No way. You know me. I'm not the brave, reckless type."

She got up from the couch and walked slowly back toward the foyer. When she reached the front door, she turned to face him. "Thanks for stopping by. I feel...better."

"Good. Call me if you need me. And you're calling the police as soon as I leave, right?"

"I will. I promise."

He rested a hand on her shoulder, wishing he could somehow shield her from everything that threatened her. And it was more than just male protectiveness. The brief peeling away of her self-sufficiency, revealing the vulnerability beneath, stirred something in him, making it harder and harder to leave.

But that was exactly what he needed to do. In a few short weeks, his work in Florida would be finished, and he would be going home, back to his life in Memphis. More than likely, he would never see her again. And that was just the way it needed to be.

Five years ago, everything they had had come to an abrupt end—final and irreversible.

Because he burned his bridges when he didn't trust her.

And she burned hers when she walked away.

Melissa leaned against the doorjamb and watched Chris back slowly up the driveway. She hadn't intended to tell him about Eugene. And she would probably live to regret it. Maybe it was fatigue—physical and emotional exhaustion. But the moment the words spilled out, a sliver of that ever-present uneasiness seemed to drift away. And for a brief moment, she didn't feel so totally alone.

With a sigh, she closed the door and twisted the lock. Chris wanted her to trust him with her safety. At one time she had trusted him with everything, including her heart. She wouldn't make that mistake again. No matter how badly he wanted to be there to protect her, she wasn't about to let him back into her life, even on a temporary basis.

But there was one concession she *would* make. She would go to the police. The idea of Branch knowing her personal business was hard to accept. But she would do it. In fact, she would go one further.

She swung open the front door and strode across the yard. Except for the occasional doctor's appointment, her elderly neighbor was always home, often working outside. Even with all the greenery obstructing her view, Mrs. Johnson may see someone prowling around.

Melissa stepped through the gate between the two properties, and a gentle breeze followed her, blowing strands of hair against her cheek and pulling some of the stickiness from the air. Next week promised some relief, a cool front, which meant temperatures in the eighties instead of the nineties.

But Mrs. Johnson wasn't waiting for the cooler weather. She sat on her porch swing with a tall glass of iced tea, beads of sweat dotting her forehead. A dark smudge marked one wrinkled cheek, and her gardening gloves and pruning shears lay on the wooden slats beside her. Two tabby cats weaved in and out of her legs.

"It looks like you've been hard at work. Your roses are beautiful." Melissa nodded toward the bed that wrapped around the outside of the curved walkway. Perfect blooms boasting a palette ranging from the palest pink to deepest fuchsia opened their petals to the late-afternoon sun.

"Thank you, dear. I managed to get a little bit accomplished, even laid down after the craft show."

She pushed back a snowy-white curl that had fallen over one brow and picked up the gloves and pruning shears. "Have a seat, dear. You know, I probably should sell and move into something with less up-keep—one of those condo complexes for old people. But there's forty years of memories here. And they probably wouldn't let me bring my animals."

"You'd be miserable. All this is what's keeping you young."

In the driveway, a car door slammed, and after several false starts, an engine sputtered to life. It was one of those 1970s muscle cars, with a low rumble that rattled the teeth and settled in the chest. Chrome headers, polished to a mirrorlike shine, protruded from under a body sporting three different colors of paint. Four, counting the gray primer.

Mrs. Johnson shook her head. "I know he's my grandson, but I sometimes wonder if Dennis will ever grow up. I thought maybe having his own place would teach him some responsibility, even it was just an efficiency apartment over his grandmother's garage."

Melissa watched him roar up the driveway and screech to a stop at its end. She had lived next door to him for more than four months but had hardly spoken a dozen words to him. Something about him made her uneasy. Maybe it was his brooding air, as if he was put out with the whole world. Maybe it was the way he would never quite make eye contact. Or maybe it was how he sat hour after hour in the upstairs window, like some self-appointed sentry.

The piercing wail of peeling rubber announced his exit from the driveway, and Mrs. Johnson again shook her head. "He's two months behind on the rent, and now he's lost his job. He's taking an art class at the college three mornings a week, but he needs to work." She sighed and took another swallow of her iced tea. "By the way, I've really enjoyed the flowers you brought over. They're just now starting to wilt."

"I'm glad you liked them." They had occupied a place in the center of her dining room table for all of a few hours. She had tried. But every time she walked through the room, her chest clenched. What should have been a thing of beauty was a constant reminder that no matter what she did or where she went, she could never let down her guard. So she had given the arrangement to Mrs. Johnson to enjoy. "Actually, that's why I'm here. Someone's watching me, and I was hoping you'd let me know if you see anyone snooping around."

"Oh, no." Concern filled her features, deepening the lines crisscrossing her face. "I haven't noticed anyone, but I'll definitely keep my eyes open. And if you ever need anything, Dennis and I are just a phone call away." She pushed herself from the swing and hobbled with the shears to her freshly tended rose bed. When she straightened, she held five long stems. "Here are some flowers you can enjoy—they

# SIX

"Derrick, have you ever known Donna to not show up for work?"

Derrick put the credit card slip he held with the others and closed the drawer. "No, she never misses."

Chris frowned, vague uneasiness nibbling at his mind. Maybe it was nothing. Maybe she was sick. But she should have called. Especially since the only number he had for her had been disconnected. Anyone else, he wouldn't have given it a second thought—a lot of people no longer had land lines. But this was Donna, and the disconnected phone line, on top of everything else, didn't look good.

"Check this out, Mr. J." Sam stepped down from the ladder and slid it to the side, offering a clear view of the window display she had just finished. A kayak hung diagonally, complemented by an interesting arrangement of paddles, a dry-top-and-pants set and miscellaneous fishing gear.

He nodded his approval at his newest employee. She was Sam, not Samantha, something she had made clear within moments of joining the Jamison Marine team. Sam fit her better, anyway. With jet-black hair in a short bob and energy enough for all three of them, she seemed like a Sam. He couldn't get her to call him Chris, but he had finally convinced her to shorten Mr. Jamison to Mr. J.

"I've got an hour till I have to leave for algebra. What else do you want me to do?"

He thought for a moment. "An order came in yesterday from U.S. Marine that we haven't had a chance to unpack yet. How about working on that?"

"Okay, Mr. J."

He watched her head toward the back of the store, hauling the ladder with her. Hiring Sam had been one of his good decisions. He had to work around the classes she was taking at the community college, but the customers loved her, and no matter what he gave her to do, she jumped right in without complaint.

Which was more than he could say for Donna. She had to be threatened with unemployment to produce some simple financial statements. Unless something changed in the next week, he was going to have to fire her. Although it probably wouldn't be necessary. She was likely already gone. If he was lucky, no Jamison Marine funds had gone with her.

By lunchtime, a solid knot of worry had formed in his stomach. He had to check on her.

"Derrick, I'm going to run some errands and pick up lunch while I'm out." He wouldn't say anything to

Derrick or Sam just yet, in case he was wrong. "Do you want me to get you anything?"

"No, I'm getting ready to nuke some frozen lasagna."

Sam leaned over the box she had carried from the back and, in one easy swipe, sliced the tape sealing its top. "I'm hitting the drive-through on my way to school."

Thirty minutes later, the knot in his stomach was bigger than when he left. He had knocked on Donna's door twice and rang her bell three times before soliciting the help of the manager, whose initial response was a solid no. She was a tough old bird, probably from years of dealing with incessant complaints and deadbeat tenants. The steel-gray eyes, pinched lips and severe haircut conjured up images of Nazi Germany, making the pen and clipboard she carried seem out of place. A more fitting prop would be an MP40 perched against her shoulder.

But here he was, standing next to her, getting ready to enter Donna's apartment. The only thing that had swayed her was the possibility that her tenant had fallen and was lying on the floor, bleeding and unconscious—possibly creating a big stain on the carpet.

She turned the key in the lock, pushed the door open and stepped inside. "Hello! Management. Anyone home?"

He started to follow, but she held up her hand. "Wait here." The rigid jaw was enough to bring him to a dead stop, even without the stern tone. He waited at the open door while she disappeared behind a small wall separating the entry from the rest of the condo. Then she walked through the apartment, calling Donna's name, her raspy voice like a file over sandpaper. It gradually faded as she moved toward the back.

He shifted his weight from one foot to the other, unable to stand still. There was too much at stake. One little peek. She would never know. He stepped around the dividing wall, and the knot in his stomach became a boulder. The living room was cleaned out; there was nothing left except indentations in the carpet where furniture had sat. The kitchen was the same—not a plate, cup or piece of silverware left behind.

And that was how she found him, standing in the kitchen, hand on an open cabinet door.

"What are you doing in here? I told you to stay outside."

Her voice wasn't raised. It didn't have to be. Her displeasure alone sent him scurrying for the door. How could one cranky five-foot-tall woman leave a grown man quaking in his boots? By the time she finished checking the unit, he was really kicking himself. He needed her help, something he would have been hard pressed to get *before* ticking her off.

"Donna is my bookkeeper," he began, as she closed and locked the door. He went on to explain, while she listened without comment. Maybe she was softening. No, that would be stretching it. But she hadn't thrown him off the property yet.

"Have you reported this to the authorities?"

"I don't have enough to formally accuse her, but after all this, I'm inclined to think the worst."

She turned to walk back to the office, and he fell in beside her. Somewhere in the distance, a motor cranked up. "You should never give someone that much free rein."

He didn't need anyone to kick him for the mess he was in. He was doing plenty of that himself. "I know. She's been my dad's bookkeeper for the past eight years, and he trusted her one hundred percent." He laughed, a dry, humorless sound. "I guess father *doesn't* always know best."

They turned the corner and found the source of the motor. A man in a maintenance uniform was hard at work with a pole saw. Several palm fronds lay scattered around his feet. When he saw his boss, he hurried to shut the machine off.

"Clayton, did you know the Andersons left, 413B?"

"No, ma'am, I didn't."

"That's what I thought." She swung open the office door and held it for Chris to enter.

"I take it her lease wasn't up?" he asked.

"No, they still had another three months. They left during the night, or I would have known." She circled around behind the desk and sat. "If there's any chance she embezzled, you'd better get it reported. And you might need this."

He looked down at the business card she handed him. Priscilla Hammond. Priscilla? She didn't look like a Priscilla. More like a Hilda or Gertrude. Maybe her tough shell was a carryover from growing up with the nickname Prissy. "Thank you, Ms. Hammond. There's a good chance the police will be in touch with you."

She acknowledged his thanks with a nod and a grunt, then turned her attention to the papers stacked on her desk, effectively dismissing him. With one last glance at the top of her bowed head, he strode from her office. He had to go to the authorities. But not without proof. And that proof was in the form of piles of handwritten ledgers. Just the thought sent waves of dread washing over him. One college accounting class was all it had taken to realize he was much better suited to police work than business. Debits and credits made his head hurt.

The first task would be removing Donna as a signer on the bank account. Large checks required a second signature—it said so on the checks. But anything under five thousand dollars, Donna had signing authority.

The next step would be advertising for an experienced bookkeeper.

He was going to need one.

Melissa inhaled the earthy scent of the rich, black dirt and straightened to admire her work. Small green plants stood full and healthy in their neat rows and gentle mounds. Soon the delicate yellow-and-white flowers would give way to Barbie-size replicas of the fruits and vegetables that would eventually grace her table.

There was something therapeutic about gardening, the fragrant smell of the herbs and flowers, the feel of the cool, moist earth on her fingers, the inspiring display of the miracle of life. Her passion for gardening started two years ago with a single potted tomato plant and had expanded each season since, one container at a time. Now, two four-by-twelve boxes allowed her hobby full expression. The boxes were already there. All she had to do was add organic fertilizer and plants.

She glanced at her watch and began stuffing the plucked sprigs of grass into the trash bag at her side. In a few short minutes, daylight would be pushed away by impending night. She picked up her pace, trying to quell her rising uneasiness. The broken window had a logical explanation. So did the apparition in the middle of the night. Maybe even the note was a prank.

But the closer it got to dusk, the greater her apprehension, and no amount of explaining was going to change that. She cast a nervous glance over her shoulder, suddenly anxious for the safety of the house. Now that the sun was down, the temperature seemed to have fallen several degrees. Or maybe that chill was coming from inside.

In one smooth motion, she hefted the bag over her

shoulder, straightened and spun around—right into a hard male body. She gasped and stumbled backward, landing on top of the bag in an unladylike sprawl.

"Sorry. I didn't mean to scare you."

The breath she had just sucked in was expelled in a whoosh, but her taut muscles relaxed only slightly. It was Dennis Johnson. His stocky frame filled her vision as he leaned over her, one hand extended to help her up. When her gaze flicked to his other hand, panic spiraled through her.

It held an envelope. Just like what was left on her front door.

She rolled from the trash bag and backed away, mind screaming its denial of the proof right in front of her. What little hope she had held out that the note was a practical joke died a sure and quick death. She was being stalked, and her stalker was Dennis.

"Relax, lady. I'm just bringing you this." He took a step toward her, and his hand shot out with the offending item.

She jumped away as if it was poisonous. She didn't want to read any more notes. She just wanted to curl into a tight ball with the comforter pulled snugly over her head and find that place where all was peace and safety and no one meant her any harm. But Dennis stood between her and the house.

"Look, I'll just lay it right here." He bent to place the envelope on the edge of one of the planter boxes. "It was left in my grandmother's box by mistake."

His words penetrated her swirling thoughts. His

grandmother's box? What was he talking about? She dropped her gaze to the envelope waiting atop one of the two-by-twelve's framing her garden. The Tampa Electric logo occupied the upper left-hand corner, and a computer-generated name and address showed through the clear plastic window in the center. It was only the utility bill. All her personal mail came to a post office box, but the Tylers' electric bill still came to the house.

She bent to retrieve it, silently chiding herself for being so paranoid. When she straightened to apologize to Dennis, he had already turned and started back across the yard toward his grandmother's place.

"Thank you," she called to his retreating figure.

Although he didn't turn, his response floated back to her on the quiet evening breeze. "Lady, you need to get some help."

Maybe he was right.

He kicked a small downed limb then continued across the yard. Before coming to Harmony Grove, he had played high school football. Then he got into trouble and got kicked off the team. According to his grandmother, he had walked around with a chip on his shoulder ever since.

She watched him disappear through the gate, then she plopped the trash bag onto the concrete patio. A green hose snaked to a sprinkler some twenty feet from the garden. No sense running a whole zone of the automatic system to cover a ten-by-twelve area. She turned the valve, and pressure filled the hose with a controlled hiss. Just as she straightened, her phone began to vibrate in her back pocket. She wiped her hands on her jeans and put the phone to her ear.

"This is your weekly checkup call."

The friendly male voice caused a flutter in her stomach, along with a touch of annoyance. "Don't you mean daily?"

"Those others weren't calls."

No, they weren't. Sunday he was on her doorstep by the time she got home from church, and Monday and Tuesday he dropped by, too. "Well, I'm fine. Just finished weeding my garden."

"You're outside?" He didn't sound pleased. "You shouldn't be outside after dark."

Annoyance flared anew. At twenty-five years old, she didn't need to be told what she should and shouldn't do. "It's not after dark. It's just now dusk." Well, maybe a little after dusk. The dazzling display of sunset had faded some time ago, and the western horizon glowed with a faint luminescence, clinging to those final moments of daylight before succumbing to darkness.

"Any more notes or gifts or anything?"

"Not a one." She stepped through the kitchen door and locked it behind her. "Isn't it a little late to still be at the store? I thought you guys closed at six."

"We do. I'm working on paperwork. You know how that goes."

Something wasn't right. She could hear it in his

voice, as if he was trying too hard to sound cheery. "Is everything okay?"

"Everything's fine. Why?"

He couldn't fool her. She knew him too well. "You don't sound fine. What's going on?"

Her question was followed by a long, heavy silence. When he finally spoke, his tone was solemn. "I lost my bookkeeper today. She split."

Was that all? It was hardly the end of the world. "I'm sure you can find someone to replace her. There are enough people out of work right now."

"That's not what I'm worried about. I've been pushing for computerized financial statements since I got here. I think I know now why she kept stalling."

"You think she was embezzling?"

"That's what it looks like. I got back to the store and started looking for the financials, and nothing has been entered. She's been stringing me along."

His discouragement struck a chord in her, and for half a second she considered dropping everything and running to the store, if for nothing more than to offer moral support. Then she checked herself. Their lives were becoming way too entangled. A month ago she was never going to see him again. Now she had been rooked into daily contact.

"I don't know how bad it is," he continued. "I've gone over the past few months' bank statements, and there aren't any big withdrawals. So if she's been taking money, it's been in small increments. I've removed her name from the checking account. But it'll be a while before I can sift through everything."

"Since there's nothing obvious, maybe any damage will be minimal."

"Maybe," he answered hesitantly. "But I don't feel good about this at all."

His usual optimism was gone, smothered beneath a heavy blanket of discouragement, and she was once again struck with that urge to run over there and do something stupid, like wrap him in another spontaneous embrace. She shook off the thought. Encouragement offered over the phone was a whole lot safer. "I'll pray that everything works out okay."

"Pray?"

She smiled. That had slipped out as naturally as talking about the weather. BethAnn was rubbing off on her. "God's an important part of my life now." Not that she had been an atheist before. She knew God was out there somewhere. She just didn't think that had a whole lot to do with her. And as long as she was kind to animals and didn't kill anybody, she would make it.

"So you *do* have some other surprises. How did that come about?"

"BethAnn. I liked the changes I saw in her. It seems like no matter what she's going through, she always has this peace about her. Well, I finally decided to go to church with her and check it out for myself. I learned that God isn't just some distant, way-out-there force. He's close and personal and cares about every aspect of our lives."

Chris was silent for several moments. He was either letting her words sink in or searching for the smoothest way to change the subject. Finally he spoke. "Well, since you've got a direct line to the Big Man Upstairs, put in a good word for me, will you?"

"I'll do that."

"And it probably wouldn't hurt to throw in a few for yourself."

"Believe me, I do. All the time."

"You should let me stay with you."

"You're not moving in here." She didn't need a bodyguard. Especially one whose rich, smooth voice and warm gaze sent a steady barrage of cannonballs slamming into her defenses. "I'll be fine. Everything's locked and I'm in for the night." Except for shutting off the sprinkler. But she wouldn't mention that.

"Maybe I can just come over and hang out. What are you doing tonight?"

"Working on transcription."

"What about tomorrow night?"

"Going to the mall with BethAnn."

"And Friday night?"

She smiled at the exaggerated eagerness in his tone. "Washing my hair."

Laughter roared through the phone. "Okay, okay, I get the hint."

She snapped the phone shut, shaking her head.

His overprotectiveness was about to drive her nuts. But it was hard to stay annoyed with him for long.

Why did he have to be so doggone charming? If she wasn't careful, she was going to find herself right back where she'd been five years ago: head-over-heels in love and poised for yet another heartbreak.

And she just wasn't willing to go there.

# SEVEN

"Hey, isn't that Chris?"

Melissa followed BethAnn's extended finger and craned her neck to see around the four teenagers coming toward them. They walked abreast, multiple piercings, heavy bling and colored, spiked hair proclaiming their individuality—or their rebellion. The mall was crowded for a Thursday night.

The teenagers passed and, sure enough, there was Chris. She heaved an exasperated sigh. "What are you doing here?"

"My assistant manager is getting married Saturday, and I had to buy a gift." He held up a large department-store bag with a bulky box inside.

She put her hands on her hips and nailed him with a stern gaze. "You knew we were going to be here, and don't try to deny it."

"You said the mall. You didn't say *which* mall."

"Knowing this is the only mall within thirty minutes of Harmony Grove, I'm sure it wasn't hard to figure out."

He broke into a teasing grin. "Hey, I really did

have a wedding gift to buy. But you can't blame me for checking on you every chance I get."

"As you can see, I'm fine." She began moving toward the exit.

"Let me follow you home. It's late."

She tensed. "I don't need you to follow me. I'm dropping BethAnn off, then going straight from the car to the house. I'll be fine."

"I won't stay," he argued. "I just want to make sure you get in okay."

"I said I'll be fine." She spaced out the words, not even trying to keep the annoyance out of her tone. She had agreed to an occasional phone call. Everything else was getting on her last nerve.

BethAnn held up an index finger. "I'm going to hit the restroom before we head out."

Melissa turned back to Chris. "I don't need you hovering over me."

"I'm only doing this because I'm worried about you." His voice was low, its smooth timbre like warm oil over her frayed nerves. He stared down at her, concern flowing from his eyes, and she turned away. She didn't want him to care, didn't want to see the warmth in that dark gaze. But there it was, reaching out to her, touching something deep inside. And for just a moment, she felt cherished.

Then he continued. "I can't help it. It's in my blood. You've got some nutcase stalking you, and coming home alone at night isn't safe."

His words brought her up short. Of course it was

in his blood—stamped into him through months at the academy and years on the force. His concern for her was the same as it was for any woman he was sworn to protect. No more, no less.

She turned away, defenses still intact, and began walking down the corridor. "I'm fine. It was one stupid little note, almost a week ago. You're over-reacting."

"I'm not overreacting. You're in danger and choosing to ignore it. What if the notes and gifts are from Eugene? What if he's found you and is getting some kind of sick thrill out of tormenting you? And what happens when that isn't enough anymore? What will he do then?"

Cold tendrils of fear slithered through her at his words, wrapping their icy grip around her heart. She shook her head. "No, it's not Eugene. He couldn't have found me. I took too many precautions."

She suddenly stopped walking and stood stock-still, a chill sweeping over her for an entirely different reason. "You said Eugene. How do you know his name?"

Something almost imperceptible flashed across his features, visible only in a slight widening of his eyes and a twitch of his lips. But it didn't light there long. A nanosecond later, the mask of control was firmly back in place. "You told me, remember?"

"I told you I had been stalked. I didn't tell you his name." She studied him, eyes narrowed. "You had me checked out. You used your connections to get information about me."

"I had to know what kind of danger you were in, but you wouldn't talk to me. Melissa, I'm sorry."

He reached out to put a hand on her shoulder, but she jerked away before he could make contact. "Don't touch me."

Next to her, a worker lowered a metal gate, shutting down her store for the night. Others began to follow suit, and Melissa stalked away, the rattle and scrape of metal closing in on her from both sides. She maintained a fast, furious walk, wishing she could just hit the door and keep running—away from the constant fear that Eugene was going to find her, and away from the oppressive overprotectiveness of Chris. He was smothering her. And he had violated her privacy. She wouldn't tell him when he first asked, so he got the information his own way.

Within moments, he was again beside her. "Melissa, please don't be angry. I'm trying to protect you."

"I don't want your protection. I want you to leave me alone." She skidded to a stop. "You had no business digging into my personal affairs."

"Okay, I shouldn't have done that. I should have waited until you were ready to tell me. I made a mistake. So how long are you going to refuse help?"

Another gate rattled downward, and a young couple overtook them, glancing back as they passed. She lowered her voice to an angry hiss. "As long as it takes. Eventually you'll go back to your own life and stay out of mine."

She spun away from him and stalked back in the direction from which they had come. BethAnn was up ahead, moving slowly toward them.

"I don't know if I'll be leaving." The words came from somewhere behind her. "I might just decide to stay here."

She stopped and whirled to face him. Surely he wasn't serious. For several moments she studied him. Finally she shrugged. "Do what you want. Just stop hounding me."

"I hope your stubbornness doesn't get you killed." He turned and walked away, down the corridor, out the door and into the night.

Now maybe he would quit bothering her. She didn't want his help. She had taken care of herself since she was nine years old. She was used to it.

So why did she feel so totally alone?

"I take it that didn't go well."

She started at BethAnn's voice so close to her ear. "He had me checked out. Before I even told him about Eugene, he already knew."

"He could probably tell something was up and wanted to find out what." Her tone was nonchalant. Of course, BethAnn wasn't the one whose privacy had been invaded. "You know," she added, "he's really worried about you."

"It's professional concern, nothing more. He's a cop. It's in his blood." He even said so.

"I've seen the way he looks at you. What he's feeling is a lot more than professional concern."

"You're seeing things that aren't there." She stepped into the night air and briskly rubbed her arms. As promised, a cool front had provided temporary relief from the oppressive heat. With the sun down and the erratic breezes, it was almost chilly.

BethAnn put one hand on her hip. The other held her purchases. "And I suppose you're going to deny that you feel anything for him, too."

"What I feel is irrelevant. It would never work."

"Why not?"

"Besides the fact that he blames me for our break-up? He slept with Adrianne."

"If you believe Adrianne. Personally, I have my doubts."

A blast of cool air swept through the parking lot, and a shiver shook her shoulders. Maybe Adrianne *was* lying. But it didn't matter. She didn't do second chances. "I know what I saw. Besides, he doesn't trust me any more than I trust him. And you can't have a relationship without trust."

She slid into the driver's seat and slammed the door, shutting out the chilly night breeze. If only her thoughts could be closed off so easily. "Chris is thinking of staying."

BethAnn stopped midmovement, right arm stretched across her lap, clutching the seat belt buckle. "Permanently?"

"I guess. He said he might not go back to Memphis." She rested her elbows against the steering wheel and put her head in her hands. "If he stays, I don't know what I'll do. What's kept me going these past few weeks is knowing he'll soon be gone."

BethAnn reached across the car to put a reassuring hand on her shoulder. "You'll make it. If you guys are supposed to be together, God will help you navigate the obstacles. And if you're not... Well, God will help you get through that, too."

"I wish I had your faith."

"You don't need mine. You've got your own. Give it time. Pray about it and listen for answers."

She nodded slowly. She *had* been praying. But her prayers had consisted of pleas to help her survive his remaining weeks in Florida. And that was as far as she was willing to go.

When she reached Harmony Grove, stores were dark and streets were almost empty. The soft glow emanating from the curtained windows of the homes projected a cozy sense of warmth. She eased to a stop in BethAnn's driveway, and the front door swung inward. Kevin stood silhouetted in the opening.

"Does he watch for you the whole time you're gone?"

A goofy smile spread across BethAnn's face, that same silly grin that appeared every time she thought of Kevin. "Probably."

Melissa smiled, too. She was happy for BethAnn, even if her own prospects for love were a mess. She shook her head and backed onto the deserted street.

Chris couldn't really be thinking of staying. His life was in Memphis. There was nothing for him in Florida except his father's marine store.

And her.

But that was ridiculous. He didn't want a relationship with her. Of course, BethAnn thought otherwise. But BethAnn was a hopeless romantic, seeing sparks where there were none.

Even if BethAnn was right, she wasn't interested. The memory of him in the arms of Adrianne would always be a dark, ugly stain, marring any chance they might have for happiness. What happened happened. And nothing was going to change it. Entertaining impossible dreams was a waste of time. So was crying over spilled milk.

With a sigh, she put her foot on the brake and turned onto Shadowood Lane. The long road was dark, the houses too distant to ease the feeling of seclusion. There was no moon, not even a sliver, and night hung heavy and thick. Her headlights cut a narrow swath through the darkness, temporarily holding it at bay. Then it rolled back in, pressing from all sides, swallowing her as she passed. Eventually, asphalt gave way to gravel, a chalky path through a field of obsidian.

Until six months ago, darkness didn't bother her. Neither did seclusion. Back then she would have gladly traded apartment living for quiet, peaceful nights, the nearest neighbor five hundred feet away. Back then she took security for granted.

She reached for the door handle, then hesitated, reluctant to leave the safety of her car. The porch light was on, but it wasn't much consolation—the semicircular glow barely reached beyond the porch steps. If only she could enter through the garage and avoid this whole trek up the walkway. Replacing the garage door with sliding glass doors had been a dumb idea.

She cast a final glance into the darkness and climbed from the car. The night was eerily still. The crickets had ceased their song, and the breezes that had chilled her thirty minutes earlier had moved past, leaving a deathly pall in their wake. She darted up the sidewalk, unable to shake the feeling that someone waited a short distance away, cloaked in darkness.

As she stepped onto the porch, a chill swept over her, prickling the skin on the back of her neck. An envelope was taped to the front door, her name across its front in familiar block print. With suddenly clumsy fingers, she snatched it from the door and jammed the key into the lock. The next moment, the shrubs against the house rustled. Strength drained from her like water, turning her limbs to gelatin. The fear nibbling at her insides threatened to explode into full-blown panic. One more lock. She had to get inside.

There was another rustle. Extended. Coming closer. Something—or someone—was moving through the bushes.

*Dear God, help me!*

She jammed the key into the upper lock and turned. It stuck for a fraction of a second. Then the dead bolt slid. She reached for the doorknob, hands shaking and heart pounding in her throat. A few more seconds…

A feline screech pierced the still night, and two cats charged from the bushes and disappeared into the darkness, one chasing the other. She stumbled into the foyer, squelching the scream rising in her throat. It was only Mrs. Johnson's cats. No one was after her. She leaned against the locked door for several moments, eyes closed and breath coming in short gasps. When she opened her eyes, Smudge peered at her from the living room doorway. She picked him up and offered several reassuring strokes down his back, allowing the last of the tension to drain from her body.

The cat incident was easy to ignore. The envelope in her hand wasn't. She put Smudge on the floor and ripped the seal, torn between curiosity over what was inside and the desire to remain blissfully ignorant. It was a single page, folded in thirds, filled with the same bold, black print as the earlier letter.

*Melissa, my sweetheart. My world is a roller coaster watching you come and go. You leave, and mournful gray clouds overshadow the sky. You return, and the sun shines again.*

*I won't ask if you enjoyed the flowers. I know what you did. You gave them away. Your rejection of my carefully chosen gift breaks my heart. I will keep working to win your love, and some-*

*day you will feel as I do. Then we will run away*
*to our own private paradise. Until then, I will*
*love you from afar.*

She dropped the page onto the Bombay chest and
clutched the doorjamb for support. She was definitely being stalked. Now there was no denying it.
This unnamed someone didn't just know what time
she went to bed last Friday night. He saw her take
the flowers to Mrs. Johnson and had been watching
her come and go ever since.

One possibility sat solidly in her mind. Dennis.
From his vantage point, he could see everything without even leaving his room. Each time she turned on
her bedroom light, then turned it off to retire for the
night. Every visit to his grandmother. Saturday evening she paraded the bouquet of roses right past him,
not giving it a second thought.

And all the while he watched from upstairs.

Bile filled her stomach and tried to push its way
up her throat. It was happening again. She had fled
Atlanta to escape one stalker, only to fall prey to
another. She should go to the police, then proceed
with getting a restraining order. It wouldn't end until
she did.

And sometimes it didn't end then.

She removed her phone from her purse, but
couldn't bring herself to dial the three numbers.

What if she was wrong?

What if she accused Dennis and then found out it was someone else?

Chris walked into his office and settled behind the scuffed oak desk. Melissa had slipped in and out of his thoughts all day, and he was no less annoyed with himself at midafternoon than he had been that morning. How could he have let Eugene's name slip? He knew she would be furious. And her reaction was just what he expected. She wanted nothing more to do with him.

And that left him feeling oddly bereft.

His visits with her had become the high point of his day. Without even realizing it, his goal had gradually shifted from simply protecting her to something much more. She was unwittingly winding her way right back into his heart, and he wasn't ready for his time with her to end. Eventually it would have to. Eventually he would go back to his life in Memphis, and she would continue hers in Harmony Grove. When that time came, he wanted everything to be all right between them.

Tonight he would call her. And he would do whatever it took to make amends, not just for his invasion of her privacy, but for all the mistakes he made five years ago. It was time to say the things that needed to be said, to tell her why he believed the worst, why he made his accusations that night. It wouldn't excuse what he did. But she would finally know what was behind his mistrust.

Derrick poked his head through the open doorway, interrupting his thoughts. "There's a call for accounts payable on line one. With Donna gone, I guess that's you."

Not for long. He had done two interviews that morning. The first candidate hadn't impressed him at all. He didn't expect a business suit, but jeans, a tank top and flip-flops didn't exactly scream *professional*. Neither did the big wad of gum that she popped as a prequel to every answer.

The second applicant, though, had been just the ticket. Karen was proficient, professional and had one hundred times the personality of Donna, which was good since he had made the position full-time and included counter sales. She was available to start Monday, which would be none too soon. He had set up online banking and printed the last six months of checks and bank statements. But after two hours of wading through handwritten notes scrawled onto journal pages, he had given up.

He took the phone from Derrick and put it to his ear. And the next two minutes went from bad to worse as he learned of one unpaid invoice after another, going back ninety days. What started as a small knot of uneasiness in his gut rapidly evolved into a cannonball.

"You've been a good customer," she explained, "but I'm afraid all future orders will have to be C.O.D. until these past-due invoices are paid."

He asked her to fax them and promised to pay as

soon as possible. Then he hung up the phone and slouched in the chair. If Donna had simply stopped paying their most important vendor, how many others had she failed to pay? Just how serious a financial mess was he in?

Suddenly he sat up straight, decision made. Until that moment, it was just an idea niggling at the back of his mind, easy to ignore. Now it screamed at him, demanding his attention. And he knew without a doubt what he would do.

The store was his father's legacy, what he had worked for all his life. Walking away now felt like turning his back on the old man. And he just couldn't do it.

He opened the desk drawer and began fishing for a card he had placed there. He had some calls to make. Before the afternoon was over, Lakeland would have one less business for sale. And Memphis would be short a detective.

He was home. And this time it was to stay.

He would do right by his father yet.

# EIGHT

Melissa slammed the dryer door and eyed the stacks of folded clothes on the table. Her favorite nightgown was missing. She specifically remembered putting it in the clothes hamper. But the last of the laundry was dried and folded, and the silk teddy seemed to have disappeared into thin air. If she didn't know better, she would swear the house was haunted.

This was the third item in less than a week. The day before yesterday it was the novel she had been reading. And Sunday, her MP3 player walked off. For someone who lived by the adage "A place for everything with everything in its place," she was sure losing a lot of things.

A familiar ringtone sounded on her phone, cutting into her private gripe session. Beethoven's Fifth. BethAnn. She hurried to the kitchen and snatched the phone from the counter.

"You sound frustrated. What's up?" BethAnn could always pick up on her moods. "Nothing serious. The dryer just ate my nightgown."

"That's a bummer. Mine eats socks. I have two

feet, so I know two socks go in, but way too often, only one comes out. I think if you ever took my dryer apart, in the bowels of the thing you'd find some mischievous little gremlin guarding a huge mound of socks."

Melissa laughed. "I'm glad I'm not the only one."

"So what are you up to?"

"Other than going crazy because I can't remember where I put anything? Not much." She peered into the oven. Her casserole had another fifteen minutes. Dinner was late, and Smudge wasn't happy. He paced back and forth in front of his empty food dish, gold-eyed gaze settling pleadingly on her face.

She lowered her voice, her tone serious. "When I got home last night, there was another note on my door."

"Oh, no. Like before?"

"Yep. He knows I gave the flowers away."

BethAnn gasped. "That's sooooo creepy. I hate to say this, but I can't stop thinking about Eugene."

"It just doesn't fit." She popped open a can of cat food, propping the phone against her ear with her shoulder. "Finding me, making the trip down here—it takes money. As long as I knew him, he never worked, just got checks from the government."

"He's on disability?"

"I think so. He only mentioned it once, and I didn't pry. He didn't look disabled. But he did say something once about being on medication."

"Maybe his problem isn't physical. A lot of mentally ill people act completely normal as long as they're medicated. But when they go off their medication, watch out."

She pulled a spoon from the drawer and nodded slowly. Maybe that was what had happened, how he'd gone from slightly quirky to terrifyingly nuts in a two-month time span. His version of reality was entertaining when he'd been telling his tales of adventure. But when he'd started seeing her as "his woman" and threatened any guy who so much as looked at her, it wasn't so entertaining anymore. Soon none of the guys in the complex had wanted to get within twenty feet of her. Even the women had given her a wide berth after some cold glares from Eugene.

"So did you call the cops about the note?"

"I sure did. Just my luck, I got Chief Branch again. He can never resist making some snide comment. This time it was something about wasting the town's resources."

"He's so full of himself."

"I know." She placed Smudge's dish on the floor and leaned back against the counter. "All us peons are beneath—"

A startled gasp choked off the rest of her words, and her heart momentarily stopped.

"Melissa?" Panic laced BethAnn's tone. "What's wrong?"

She stood frozen, eyes glued to the window behind the kitchen table. A moment earlier, a face was framed in one of the panes, dimly illuminated by the patio light. The instant she saw it, it was gone.

"Someone was just looking in my window."

"Call the cops. I'll be there in a few minutes."

"He'll be gone, especially if he sees me calling them." And if she called Chief Branch out again so soon, he'd probably try to arrest her.

"Do it inconspicuously. You know, act relaxed, like you're talking to me."

She turned her back to the window and, with hands shaking, dialed 9-1-1. Even after disconnecting the call, she kept the phone pressed to her ear. Moments later, the face reappeared, nothing more than an indistinct shape. The sheers hanging at the window and the dimness of the patio light made her prowler impossible to identify.

But she was probably quite visible under the bright kitchen lights. Uneasiness washed over her, a sense of total vulnerability. She resisted the urge to run and hide and forced herself to continue her pretend conversation—talking, laughing, even gesturing for effect. Her performance could have won an Emmy… until the phone began to ring in her hand.

It was Chris. But his greeting was interrupted by a high-pitched shout from outside. *BethAnn?*

"I've gotta go." She blurted the words and snapped the phone shut, not giving him a chance to protest. In the foyer, the frosted sidelight strobed red and blue, and she heaved a sigh of relief. Just as she opened the door, a Harmony Grove police vehicle ground to a halt. BethAnn's van sat in front of it, driver's door wide open. Where was BethAnn?

Alan jumped from the car. "Freeze!" he commanded, pistol leveled on some point across the yard. "Hands in the air."

She started at the sharp command and followed his gaze to where a lone figure stood at the far end of the house, dimly silhouetted against the dappled glow of Mrs. Johnson's garage light.

A female voice called out. "Alan, it's me. He ran that way." She lowered her hands and pointed behind her. "Jumped the fence onto Mrs. Johnson's property."

*BethAnn? What was she doing over there?*

Alan shot across the yard, while BethAnn headed toward the front door. At the porch she paused to catch her breath. "When I got out of the car, someone was coming out from behind the house. The instant he saw me, he ducked back and took off across the yard."

Melissa scowled at her. "I can't believe you chased him. What did you plan to do with him if you caught him?"

BethAnn held up her keys. A mini canister of mace dangled from the key ring. "I knew the police would get here any minute, and I figured I could disable him in the meantime."

"I appreciate the thought, but I don't want you getting hurt on my account. I'd rather you stick with running BethAnn's Fabrics and leave the police work to the professionals."

"I know. This was just too tempting."

Melissa shook her head. BethAnn always was the impulsive one. Age hadn't taken it out of her. Neither had marriage.

When Alan walked across the front yard a few minutes later, he was alone. "I didn't find anyone." He pocketed the flashlight, removed a pad and pen and addressed BethAnn. "Describe the person you saw."

"Well, I didn't get that close. He started to come out from behind the house but saw me and ran. He was a stocky build, between five-nine and six foot. I think he was wearing jeans and a T-shirt, but I couldn't say what color."

Alan turned to Melissa. "Any idea who it was?"

"Not really. Stuff has been going on for a week now. It started with two creepy notes, and now this."

"Tell me about the notes."

"I'll do better than that. I'll show them to you." She opened the door and motioned him inside. She liked Alan. He treated each call with the seriousness of a murder investigation. Which was more than she could say for his chief.

Alan read both notes, then lifted his gaze, brown eyes grave. "Any idea who wrote these?"

She drew in a deep breath. "Possibly."

BethAnn stepped up beside her, lending silent encouragement, and Alan wrote feverishly in his notepad. When she had finished, he closed the pad and slid it back into his shirt pocket. "Show me which window he was at, and I'll try to lift some prints. I'd like to take these notes into evidence, too."

She led him through the kitchen and out the back door. Regardless of what Chris thought, Alan was good. What he lacked in experience, he made up for in eagerness. By the time he finished, fine black powder coated the outside of the kitchen window and peppered the stucco sill beneath.

"If anything else happens, give us a call. Meanwhile, I'll drive by here regularly."

She walked with him and BethAnn down the sidewalk as another set of headlights cut a path up the driveway. *Not again.*

BethAnn grinned widely. "It's Chris. So we'll be leaving you in capable hands." She skipped to her van and turned back for one final wave. The grin was still there.

Melissa shook her head. If she left BethAnn in charge of her love life, she and Chris would be married before year's end.

Chris jumped from his Blazer and reached her in two long strides. "Are you okay?"

"I'm fine. What are you doing here?"

He ignored the annoyance in her tone. "After the way you answered the phone, I think that's obvious." His gaze circled the yard, but nothing seemed out of the ordinary, at least in front. "So what happened here?"

"Nothing serious." She dropped her gaze to the ground and shifted her weight onto one heel-clad foot. She obviously hadn't changed her clothes after work. The charcoal-gray tailored suit had *professional* written all over it. And her stance was about as relaxed as her dress. She stood straight and stiff, arms crossed protectively in front of her. What would it take to penetrate that shell of self-sufficiency that had only grown thicker over the years?

"I'm guessing BethAnn didn't just drop by for a visit."

Several moments passed while he waited for her to answer. Finally she drew in a deep breath. "I was on the phone with her and thought I saw someone looking in the kitchen window. It was probably nothing."

He clenched his teeth against the sense of protectiveness surging up from within. If only she would let him stay. But she had already flat-out refused. And that was before she was furious with him. He bit back the words of caution hovering on the tip of his tongue. "If anything happens that makes you at all uncomfortable, you know you can call me any time."

Her stance didn't relax in the slightest. She was more closed off than ever. "Thanks, but that's what the police are for."

He heaved a heavy sigh. He had really blown it. He was amazingly good at that, at least where Melissa was concerned. "Well," he began, "my reasons for calling were more than just checking on you. I wanted to apologize for getting my partner involved. You were going to tell me when you were good and ready, and I let concern get in the way of my better judgment."

She momentarily lifted her gaze to his face, then let it once again fall to the gravel drive. But in those brief moments, her features seemed to soften just a little. Finally she shrugged. "Don't worry about it. What's done is done."

"I know it is, but I was hoping you'd give me a chance to make it up to you." Actually, he had a lot more to make up for than his invasion of her privacy. His refusal to trust her had almost destroyed them both. He squared his shoulders, searching deep inside for the strength to say what needed to be said and the confidence that the words would somehow be enough.

"Missy," he began, "I know I've said I'm sorry for everything that happened five years ago, but I can't begin to tell you how much I've regretted the choices I made. I should never have listened to Adrianne's lies."

"Adrianne's lies?" She met his gaze fully, brows drawn together. "What did she tell you?"

"The whole time you and I were together, she was always dropping hints about Lance."

A hardness crept into her eyes. "If I had wanted Lance, I wouldn't have left him in the first place. It was you I was in love with."

"I know that now. But she was constantly insinuating there was something going on between you. Since she was your best friend, I had no reason to doubt her."

Her eyes narrowed, and pain flickered in their depths. "But you doubted *me*."

"I did, and that's something I'll kick myself for until the day I die." He drew in a slow breath. It was time to tell her the whole story. Maybe she would understand. "The night you walked in, she had stopped by my apartment while you were at school. I was complaining that I wasn't seeing much of you, with school and work and all the wedding plans. Well, she started acting really uncomfortable, as if there was something she knew but didn't want to tell me." He stopped speaking for several moments and closed his eyes. Five years later, the memory still felt like a steel fist clamping down on his heart.

"Anyway, I got this sick feeling in the pit of my stomach and asked her point-blank if you were seeing someone. She wouldn't answer me, just looked at the floor. But I kept pressing. Finally she told me you had been seeing Lance for the past four months and were planning to call off the wedding."

She stared at him, eyes wide and mouth agape. "And you believed her?"

"I know, it was stupid." Stupid and inexcusable. How would she ever forgive him? "She was so convincing. I was completely devastated. And, of course, she was right there ready to offer sympathy. The comforting hug was welcome. But when she planted that kiss on me the moment you walked in the door, I just froze. After what she had told me, I was too stunned to react one way or the other. Two years later, she began dating my friend Todd. I don't know if her conscience started to bother her or what, but she eventually broke down and told him everything." He shook his head, regret weighing heavy on his heart. "Believe me, when I got that phone call, I *really* wanted to die. I finally learned the truth, but it was two years too late."

She continued to stare up at him, arms wrapped tightly around her midsection, physical evidence of the wall she had put around her heart. Finally she spoke, the pain in her features at odds with the icy tone. "You could have talked to me, you know. You didn't have to start sleeping with her."

His eyes widened and his jaw sagged. "What?"

"You and Adrianne had been having your fling for quite a while. I was just lucky I found out before I made the mistake of marrying you." She spat the words at him, the pain in her eyes now mixed with anger.

Shock ricocheted through his brain. Adrianne, of all people! She was *so* not his type. Shallow, cheap, flirty and totally wrapped up in herself. The complete opposite of Melissa. "Is that what you think, that I slept with her?"

For some time, her eyes remained locked on his face, searching for answers, confidence fleeing her gaze with every passing moment. "Are you saying you didn't?"

"Of course I didn't! Why would you even think that?"

"But Adrianne—" She shook her head as if trying to wrap her mind around something just out of her grasp. "Adrianne told me that this thing between you had been going on for several months."

He sank against the side of her car, feeling like someone who had just taken a solid steel-toed boot to the gut. Adrianne hadn't just lied to him; she'd lied to Melissa, too. All this time, Melissa believed he had been unfaithful. And he hadn't done anything to dispel that notion, just accused her of cheating with Lance. No wonder she had severed ties so thoroughly.

"Whatever Adrianne told you, she was lying, just like she lied to me about Lance." Somehow he had to convince her. "What you walked in on that night is all that ever happened. You've got to believe me, Melissa."

She shook her head slowly. "I don't know what to think."

He pushed himself away from the car and rested one hand on her shoulder in silent entreaty. "All I did was accept a comforting hug. That kiss was initiated by her, right when you walked in the door. And I don't think the timing was any accident. She had it all planned out." He dropped his hand and leaned back against the car again. "There was just one thing she didn't anticipate—my reaction. After that night, she kept coming around, and all I would do was talk about you. She said I needed to forget about you, that you had made your choice and were happy with Lance. Finally she gave up."

While he talked, he studied her, searching her face for some sign that the barriers were coming down. But there was none. She never met his gaze, just stood ramrod straight, arms still crossed in front of her. Did she understand? Did she even believe him?

"Melissa," he prodded, "please talk to me."

She shook her head, all her thoughts and feelings locked securely behind that protective wall that had gone up the moment she had seen him with Adrianne. "I have to go. I need time to think."

She spun away from him, strode quickly up the walk and disappeared into the huge old house. For several moments, he stared at the closed door, doubt chasing regret through the corridors of his mind. How could something so perfect have gone so horribly wrong? How could a simple misunderstanding cause a rift so big it couldn't be spanned?

Determination surged through him. Somehow, some way, he would make everything right again. Whatever it took, he would win her back.

That was his new goal.

Second only to keeping her safe.

# NINE

Melissa backed from Kevin and BethAnn's driveway onto the short dead-end road that branched off Main Street. She hadn't planned to stay so long. But Sunday lunch after church turned into a whole afternoon of chatting and reminiscing. And, in Beth-Ann's case, pondering a future for Melissa with Chris. BethAnn had been thrilled to hear his version of what had happened that night and saw no problem with them simply picking up where they had left off.

But it wasn't that easy. No one had ever penetrated the wall around her heart. No one except Chris. And that ended in heartbreak. Even before Chris, she had been guarded. After her father left, she watched her mother make one bad choice after another. She was still making them. And so far, nothing in her own life had convinced her she would do any better than her mother had.

But what if BethAnn was right? What if God really was trying to bring them back together? If so, Friday night's discussion was a step in the right direction. There had been no affair. Not only that, but

Chris had stayed true to her even when he thought she had betrayed him. That was his version of it, anyway, one she hadn't totally bought into. It would take more than a few days to throw away everything she had believed for the past five years.

She mashed the brake to make her turn onto Shadowood Lane. She still had another two hours of daylight left. Maybe the evening would be uneventful—no notes on the door, no faces at the window and no bumps in the night. And maybe she could lose herself in a good book and pretend, at least for a short time, that the world was safe and her greatest threat was light years away.

But as she drew closer to the end of the road, the tension that had been blessedly absent all day gradually sifted back over her, and for the thousandth time, she longed for some closer neighbors. If Beth-Ann was still single, she would seriously consider having a roommate.

When she started up the long gravel drive, a black Blazer waited at its end. Chris hadn't been by since Friday night. On Saturday, manning the store and attending his assistant manager's wedding had left him with just enough time for a quick phone call, which was for the best. She had a lot to sort out, and that was going to require time away from him.

He stepped from his vehicle, holding a flat white box with a familiar green-and-red logo. "I come bearing gifts. I hope you're hungry. I stopped by Pappy's on the way in."

A heavenly aroma wafted to her on the late-afternoon breeze, and her stomach rumbled. The pot roast, potatoes and carrots that had been so good at twelve-thirty were long gone at six. Besides, nobody made pizza like Pappy.

"If you're busy, I can just leave it."

"No, you can come in. I'll share it with you." She flashed him a smile and started up the walk. The company would be nice.

"I tried to call you this morning just after opening the store. When it went to voice mail, I figured you were probably in church."

She cast a glance over her shoulder. "Yep. Sunday mornings between ten and twelve, you won't get me." She started to step onto the porch and froze, eyes locked on the nearest living room window. That all-too-familiar sense of dread settled over her.

"Is everything all right?"

"I don't know." She always kept her blinds open slightly, the slats angled downward so she could see out but no one could see in. The blinds on the living room window just to her right had slats angled in the opposite direction. "The blinds are…different."

From where she stood, the couch in front of the window was visible. As was the lamp on the end table, still illuminated from when she read her Bible and drank her morning coffee. She hadn't turned it off before she left. A light on gave the illusion that someone was home. Of course, whoever was watching her probably knew when the house was vacant.

Chris stepped up beside her, and within moments evidently noticed the same thing she had. "Wait here." He handed her the pizza and stalked to his truck. When she unlocked the door, he went in first, pistol drawn.

She followed him from room to room, much as she had done with Branch and Alan. And Chris didn't find any more than the other men had. All the windows and doors were locked, all her personal items untouched. Even the sliders were secure. With the Charley bar down and the pin in the top, no one was coming through without breaking the glass.

Chris turned from the window next to her bed, the last to be checked. "Everything's secure. What do you think happened to the blinds?"

"It had to have been me." There was no other explanation. "I cleaned the house yesterday, and I did dust those sills. I don't remember adjusting any of the blinds, but that doesn't mean anything. I'm not remembering a lot of things lately."

She walked from the room and headed toward the stairs. However the slats got turned, it was easy enough to remedy. And the sooner the better. When she reached the living room, she turned to face him. "Thank you. I'm so glad you were here. Otherwise, I would have had to call the police and risk Branch's annoyance, or come in alone and check it out myself."

"Don't ever do that." He put both hands on her shoulders, his dark gaze heavy with concern. "If you're not comfortable calling the police, call me. Don't put yourself in danger."

"But once again, it turned out to be nothing." She sighed and reached for the wand to the blinds, but he stopped her.

"Wait. I'm going to have Alan see if he can lift any prints, just in case."

She gave him a shaky smile. He was so sweet, validating her fears even though he had just proven no one had come inside. The fact was she was losing her mind—misplacing things and fiddling with the blinds with no recollection of doing so.

He reached over her head to grasp the wand near its top. Moments later the angle of those blinds matched the others in the room. "So has anything else happened? Any more notes? Creeps looking in your windows?"

"Nope, just the two notes, and no more faces at the window."

"Two notes? I only know about one."

Oh, yeah. She hadn't told him about the second one. "I had another note when I got home from the mall Thursday night."

His gaze hardened. "And what did *this* note say?"

"I don't remember exactly. I gave both notes to Alan."

There was a visible tic in his jaw now, and a vein began to throb at his temple. "I'm not looking for verbatim. A summary will do just fine."

"He let me know he's still watching me. He knew I gave the flowers to Mrs. Johnson."

"That's it." The words exploded from his mouth. "I'm not letting you stay here alone any longer."

"You're not moving in." She crossed her arms and stared up at him, daring him to argue.

"Then go stay with BethAnn."

"I can't. BethAnn is allergic to cats. Besides, all my stuff is here."

For several moments, he looked at her, indecision flashing across his features. Then he put his hands on her shoulders again and gently turned her to face him. "I'm really worried about you, Missy."

His eyes held hers, and a glow infused her chest, spreading like warm honey through her body. No one ever called her Missy except Chris. The name on his lips was an endearment, a soft caress that set her walls of resistance teetering on the brink of collapse. She tore her gaze from those riveting eyes, determined to break the cord that had snagged and now held her. It didn't help. When it wasn't his eyes or his voice, it was his scent, rugged and masculine, reminiscent of a field of evergreens with subtle hints of spice.

She shrugged off the effect, as well as his offer to help. "I'm all right. I keep everything locked, and I won't come and go alone in the dark anymore." That was a new precaution, implemented after the last note. "Alan promised to patrol, too."

He frowned but still didn't release her. His hands

were warm against her shoulders, almost as warm as his gaze. "I wish you would let me protect you. I'm staying, you know."

Staying? In Florida? Conflicting emotions did battle inside her chest. "What do you mean?"

"I faxed my resignation to the department and took the store off the market."

"Why?"

"Two reasons. First of all, the store is in serious financial trouble. Monday I'll find out just how deep. But I can't sell it in this condition, and I don't have the heart to close it down. I can't do that to Dad."

There was a hitch in his voice. She understood. She had lost a parent, too, just in a different way. Actually, she had lost two. With her father, it was overnight—he was gone when she got up in the morning. With her mother, it was a little more gradual—she withdrew into herself, sliding further and further down that path of emotional self-destruction until everything connecting her to her former life had disappeared.

She reached up to place a hand over one of his. "I'm sorry. I know this is really hard on you."

"I wish I had been here for him. But whatever it takes, I'm going to make the store a success."

"If anyone can do it, you can. I have no doubt."

He took both of her hands in his and squeezed them in silent gratitude. That appreciation was reflected in his eyes, along with something much deeper. It slid right past the protective barrier and into her heart. When she subconsciously moistened her lips, his gaze dipped to her mouth. He was thinking about kissing her. And she was trying to remember just why that was a bad idea.

Instead, he cleared his throat and flashed her a crooked grin. "We've got an out-of-this-world Pappy's Supreme getting cold on the kitchen counter."

"Well, we can't let that happen." She followed him to the kitchen, tamping down both disappointment that he didn't attempt that kiss he was obviously thinking about, and dismay that she wanted it in the first place. "You never did tell me your second reason for staying."

He raised the lid on the box and folded it backward to rest on the counter, his movements slow and deliberate. When he turned to face her, the teasing grin was gone. "To see if miracles really do happen."

She didn't need to ask what miracle he was hoping for. It was all there in his gaze. She busied herself with removing plates from the cupboard and pouring drinks. She was going to do what BethAnn suggested—be open to the possibility that God might want her and Chris together. But she needed to keep a clear head and not rush into anything. And with Chris woven so intricately into her life, that wasn't going to be an easy task.

A thousand mini hammers pounded the inside of Chris's skull and beat against the backs of his eyes.

It had been a terrible day. And he had the headache to prove it.

Karen, his new bookkeeper, had shown up at nine, as expected. She was awesome—quick and sharp, with a knack for making sense of gibberish. That was the good news.

The bad news was that every vendor that had supplied products to Jamison Marine in the past ninety days had at least one unpaid invoice, and no payroll taxes had been deposited for three months. The penalties and interest alone were going to kill him.

"Who is AA Best Marine Supply?" Karen asked.

"I'm not sure." He sat next to her, helping her sort through the mess, which was probably why his head hurt so badly. Accounting really wasn't his thing. "Why?"

"Because there have been payments to them three or four times a month as far back as I've checked."

He gave a dry, humorless laugh. "At least that's one vendor I won't be getting a call from. Maybe they're affiliated with one of my regular vendors, like a parent company or something. How much are we talking about?"

"Over the past twelve months, about a hundred and twenty thousand dollars."

When a web search turned up nothing, Karen dug deeper. "If they're a Florida company, I can find them on the Division of Corporations website." Her fingers flew over the keys, and several clicks later, she sat back in her chair. "Bingo."

Chris leaned forward to see what she had found. Nothing had come up under corporations or LLCs, but a search of fictitious name registrations produced a listing for AA Best Marine Supply. He scrolled down, reading as he went. It was a local company with a Winter Haven address. Why didn't he know who they were?

When he got to the section titled Owner Information, perplexity morphed to dread. The owner of the company was Waymon Anderson. Donna's husband. She hadn't just mishandled the money—she had stolen it. Lots of it. Now he could go to the police. If they couldn't recover enough to keep the bank from foreclosing, he would be wiped out. Everything his father had worked for, gone in a flash. He was almost glad the old man hadn't lived to see it.

All the way home, the vise in his gut competed with the one around his head until he thought he would have to pull over and throw up. Just last night, he'd asked Missy to dinner. And surprisingly, she accepted. He was to pick her up in a little over an hour. All day long he had looked forward to it, the one bright spot in his otherwise dreary day. Now he was thinking of canceling.

It wasn't just the headache. It was the whole situation. He was almost thirty years old and back where he was when he finished high school. No, he was worse off. Back then he at least had a nice chunk of cash he had saved from working part-time in his father's store. Not anymore. Now he was on the brink of financial collapse, with much of his own measly savings having gone to keep the store afloat. Why would Missy even want him? He had nothing to offer her.

But at one time, she'd loved him for who he was. When he decided he wanted to go to the police academy instead of taking over his father's marine store, she stood behind him, even though the pay would be much less. Of course, Missy had never been one for appearances. Or for extravagant possessions. But would she want someone with little more than a car and the roof over his head?

He didn't even know if he could make her happy. With a mother who'd left before he finished kindergarten and a father who'd struggled to raise him alone, what did he know of building a successful marriage?

He pulled up in front of the house where he had lived longer than half his life and stopped next to a familiar green '69 Pontiac. Betty was there. The '69 Pontiac was unique enough, but the collage of bumper stickers with their assorted messages urging drivers to save the whales, go vegan and be kind to animals made it one of a kind. She had cleaned the place for years, and he saw no reason to discontinue her services. Until today.

As soon as he walked in the door, Betty began gathering her cleaning supplies. "I'm really late today," she explained in her soft Alabama drawl. "One thing after another came up, and I just couldn't get here. I'll be back tomorrow to finish."

He laid his keys and phone on the kitchen counter and removed a gel pack from the freezer. "Don't worry about it. Go ahead and clean. I'm going to lie down and try to knock out a headache. Then I'll be gone."

He stumbled to the bedroom, leaving Betty in the midst of dusting the entertainment center. Hopefully two more heavy-duty painkillers and twenty-five minutes with an ice pack would do the trick. He really needed this night out and the brand of comfort only Missy could provide. There was something about her that made a man forget all his problems. Maybe it was those expressive blue eyes that belied the tough exterior she tried to project. Or that thick, luscious hair the color of dark chocolate and the texture of silk. Or maybe it was that quick wit and sarcastic sense of humor that seemed to always set right whatever was wrong.

He flopped onto his side and pressed the ice pack to his head, the vacuum humming softly in the distance. No matter how he felt, in twenty minutes he would get up, push aside the worries of his day and go get Missy. He had guaranteed her a relaxing evening out, and nothing was going to make him renege on that promise—not financial concerns, not his own insecurities and certainly not a headache.

# TEN

Melissa glanced at her watch for the twentieth time in the past half hour. It was exactly one minute later than the last time she looked. She heaved an impatient sigh and checked her appearance in the gilded mirror that hung over the Bombay chest, something she had done almost as many times as she had checked her watch. She wasn't vain, just apprehensive. After all, it was the first real date she had had in months.

At least that was what she assumed it was. Because no matter how she denied it, what she saw in Chris's eyes wasn't just professional concern. Sometime between his learning about Eugene and the almost-kiss in her living room last night, everything had changed. Which left her with some decisions to make. Letting him into her life could open the door to a bright and happy future...or some serious heartbreak. In her experience, one was as likely as the other.

She glanced in the mirror again and resumed her pacing, heels clicking on the hardwood floor. Hot rollers had given her already thick hair even more body, and she had taken extra care with her makeup.

The black dress pants she wore fit her well, as did the black-and-teal blouse. Strappy spike heels completed the ensemble.

But she didn't have to worry. Chris always thought she looked good, whether dressed for a night on the town or sporting a ponytail and sweatband, fresh in from working in the yard. And he had no problem with telling her so. That was something she missed.

She stopped pacing and glanced at her watch. Being late wasn't like Chris. Neither was not calling when something came up. She snatched the phone from her purse and punched in his number. Four rings later, it was answered by...*a female voice?*

"Oh, I—um—I think I have the wrong number," she stammered. "I was trying to call Chris Jamison."

"No, you have the right number." The words flowed through the phone like warm butter. It was the voice of a Southern belle, a character right off the set of *Gone with the Wind.*

She drew in a shaky breath, suddenly light-headed. Who was this woman, and why was she with Chris when he was supposed to be with *her?* "Is—is he there?"

"Yes, ma'am, but he can't come to the phone right now. Can I give him a message?"

The smooth drawl echoed in her mind, scattering her thoughts and thrusting her back to a place she didn't want to go. Images danced across her imagination, a nightmare in reverse—Adrianne's confession, Chris's accusations, and finally, the man she loved with all her heart in the arms of another woman. She squeezed her eyes shut, trying to block the flow of pictures. "No…no message."

There was nothing to say. Not now, not ever.

She laid the phone on the antique chest and leaned back against the wall, arms clutching her stomach. It couldn't be happening again. But it was. She had almost let down her guard, almost let him convince her that she didn't really see what she thought she saw.

When would she learn? Men like him were full of stories. They spun them at will to suit their fancy, telling their women what they wanted to hear, because anything else would be too painful. But the stark truth was staring her in the face. He was a womanizer, and there was no denying it. The first time she had caught him in the act. This time a phone call found him out.

Twice now he had duped her. Obviously she was a poor judge of character. In fact, she was no different from her mother. The backs of her eyes grew hot with impending tears, but she blinked them back. She wouldn't cry. He wasn't worth it.

But even without the tears, Smudge knew something was wrong. He walked back and forth in front of her, rubbing against her shins with each pass. She bent to pick him up and held him to her chest. His warmth and affection offered a measure of comfort. But as much as she loved her cat, she needed an understanding ear. If anything would lift her spirits, it would be spending her botched-up evening with BethAnn.

When she rolled to a stop in front of the small bungalow-style house, she almost changed her mind. The living room blinds were open, and BethAnn and Kevin were cuddled together on the couch, watching TV. Loneliness stabbed through her, leaving gaping holes in her heart.

For several moments, she sat with one hand on the stick shift, torn between slipping quietly away and crashing her friends' romantic evening. Then Beth-Ann made the decision for her. She suddenly looked away from the TV screen and hurried to the door.

"Hey, y'all," she called, "come on in." She stood on the porch waving with enough enthusiasm to welcome the president, not the least bit annoyed with the interruption. Then her smile faded and creases of concern moved in. "Isn't Chris with you?"

"No, he's not."

"What happened? This was supposed to be your big date."

"I know. He stood me up."

BethAnn's jaw dropped. "No way! Why?"

"I don't know. I called to talk to him and got Scarlett O'Hara."

"Let's take a walk."

Before she could argue, BethAnn told Kevin she'd be back later and closed the door.

Melissa frowned at the frozen image on the TV screen, visible through the front window. "I'm interrupting your movie."

"That's what pause buttons are for. This is important." BethAnn put an arm across her shoulder and led her down the driveway toward the park a block away. "Okay, tell me what happened."

She drew in a deep breath. "He was supposed to pick me up at six-thirty and never showed. I finally called to find out why, and a woman answered his phone."

"Any idea who she was?"

"Not a clue."

For several moments, BethAnn walked in silence, brows drawn together. They had reached the park and were working their way toward the lake at its west end. In the final lingering moments of daylight, the park was deserted except for two small groups of teenagers. At the merry-go-round, three girls squealed as two young men spun them at breakneck speed. Another young couple sat on two swings, pushing themselves in slow circles as they talked. Six years ago, that had been her and Chris on those very swings, exchanging stories, sharing dreams, planning the future. Life was simple then, so full of promise.

"At least this time I found out much earlier than three weeks before our wedding date—not that I would ever again consider marrying him."

"I wouldn't write him off just yet," BethAnn suggested. "It may be totally innocent. Like maybe the other woman is his cousin."

"I know all his cousins, and none of them are Southern belles. Just admit it. He's a womanizer, and I was stupid to even entertain thoughts of any kind of relationship with him." She crossed her arms and stared over at the lake. Three mallard ducks glided along its surface, relaxed and unperturbed by the two of them walking and talking a few yards away. Ripples fanned out as they cut a silent path through the water. What a life. No complicated relationships. No tough decisions. Just lazy days of hanging out, drifting along, soaking up the sunshine. And steering clear of the gators.

"Well," BethAnn persisted, "I'm sure there's a logical explanation. When he calls, you'll probably find out it was all a big misunderstanding."

"No, I won't. Because when he calls, I have no intention of talking to him." Over the past two and a half weeks, she had had her whole world turned on end. It was time to take back the reins of control. And if that meant never seeing Chris again, so be it.

"Don't you at least want to hear what he has to say?"

"No, I really don't, because it wouldn't make a bit of difference." She stopped suddenly and spun to face BethAnn. "Maybe there *is* a logical explanation. Maybe it's as innocent as you say. But you know what? I was actually starting to fall for him again, and I can't live like this, always wondering when I'm going to catch him with someone else." She expelled a heavy sigh and stalked down the sidewalk that circled the lake. "You thought God might be trying to bring us together. Well, I think this is God's way of showing me it would be one huge mistake."

"You could look at it that way. Or it may be the devil trying to throw a monkey wrench into God's plans. I think you need to have an open mind and keep praying about it."

She grunted a nonresponse. The answer she had was perfectly fine. If she took this canceled date as a sign she wasn't to be with Chris, she couldn't get hurt. Definitely the safest way to go.

BethAnn put a comforting hand on her shoulder. "What do you say we go back to my place for a movie? It'll take your mind off everything for a while."

Melissa forced a half smile. A movie actually sounded good.

BethAnn continued. "And let's plan something fun for this weekend. Nothing extravagant, just something to get us away from Harmony Grove for a few hours. Have you ever been to Mary Holland Park over in Bartow?"

"Not that I remember."

"Kevin and I were planning to take a picnic lunch and go out there Saturday afternoon. But I can leave him at home."

Melissa smiled again, but this time it didn't feel so forced. "I'm so glad you came back to Harmony Grove." She had friends, but none like BethAnn, who knew her almost as well as she knew herself.

"Harmony Grove has a way of luring people home."

"In your case, Harmony Grove had some help."

"Yeah," BethAnn agreed, green eyes dancing. "Kevin might have had *something* to do with it."

"I think Kevin had *everything* to do with it." Melissa looked back out over the surface of the lake, her heart a little lighter than it had been minutes earlier. "Well, if you don't mind, I'll take you up on your Mary Holland Park invitation. But Kevin can come."

"Great! We've got tonight and Saturday covered. And we'll fill up every night in between, if it'll help."

"That won't be necessary. If I took you away from Kevin that long, I think he'd go through withdrawal."

A slow smile spread across BethAnn's face. "You're probably right."

Chris opened his eyes and tried to get his bearings.

The room was dark, and he was lying on top of the bedding, fully dressed. His head felt as if it was stuffed full of cotton, his brain trying to function through a drug-induced haze. What time was it, anyway? Something was obscuring the glowing red numbers on the digital alarm clock. He reached for the nightstand, and his hand met a squishy object. An ice pack. Only it wasn't cold anymore. It wasn't even cool.

Memory returned in pieces. He'd had a headache and had lain down with the ice pack, which he had evidently thrust aside at some point. He hadn't planned on going to sleep; he was just going to lie down for twenty minutes, then…

Missy!

In one smooth stroke, he jumped to his feet and flung the ice pack on the floor. Seven-fifty! He'd promised to pick her up at six-thirty!

Phone. Where did he leave his phone? He ran through the house, flicking on lights as he went. It was on the kitchen counter, right next to his keys. He flipped it open and dialed Missy's number, hoping against hope she would let him explain. If he thought he owed her an apology before, he had some *serious* apologizing to do now.

Four rings later, her message came on, and he snapped the phone shut with a sigh. Of all the days to get a headache. If he had to lie down, why didn't he at least set the alarm, just in case? He shook his head and put the phone back on the counter. He really blew it. Missy finally agreed to go out with him, and he slept through their date! Hopefully she was just mad at him for standing her up. Because another disturbing possibility chewed at his sanity—that she opened her door, thinking it was him, and it was her stalker. How could he be so stupid? If something happened to her, he would never forgive himself.

He snatched up his keys and headed out the door. He would make the trip to Harmony Grove. If her car was there and he couldn't get her to the door, he would call Alan to check on her. She would really be ticked off then, but he would at least know she was safe.

When he reached her place, the gravel drive was

empty, the big old house dark except for a single porch light. She must have decided to go out.

Hopefully, she was alone.

He flipped open the phone and tried once more. Again, it went to voice mail. He jammed the Blazer into Reverse. As much as he wanted to apologize and make everything right, his main priority was finding her and making sure she was safe. She likely hadn't gone far. The first place he would check was BethAnn's.

When he drove past the white clapboard house and saw the gold Civic sitting in the driveway, relief washed over him. She had made it as far as Beth-Ann's, so she was in good hands. He could go home and rest easy. Except that she was still mad at him, mad enough to refuse to take his calls.

He heaved a heavy sigh and headed back to Lakeland. There was nothing else he could do. Eventually she would have to talk to him. Then he would explain. In the meantime, he would let Alan know so he could check on her more often. Doing it himself would be out of the question.

As soon as he walked into the house, he placed one last call. If she didn't take this one, he would leave a message. If he was lucky, she might actually play it back.

A whispered female voice answered the call. His heart leaped into his throat. "Missy?"

"No, it's BethAnn. Melissa's in the bathroom." She spoke in a rushed whisper. "Look, I don't have a lot of time here, so I'm going to cut to the chase. Were you with a woman?"

"What?" *Where in the world did that come from?* "I was sleeping, trying to knock out a headache." Why was he on trial?

There was a heavy sigh on the other end of the line. "I guess Melissa's right about you."

"I don't understand. What's going on?" There were lots of reasons for missing a date. Why would she assume he was with another woman?

"You've already been caught, so don't bother trying to deny it." She was still whispering, but her disdain came through loud and clear.

"There's nothing to deny. I was alone." He shook his head in disbelief. He had been tried, convicted and sentenced with no opportunity to defend himself. She had reason to be angry. He made plans then stood her up. But this other-woman stuff was totally off-the-wall. Was that what life with Missy would be like? Had that one bad experience soured her so badly that she would never trust him again?

No, he would help her work through it. Whatever it took, he would show her that he wasn't like her father, that he was faithful and committed and had eyes for no one but her. There had to be a way.

Betty! Betty could vouch for him. "If you don't believe me, I'll give you the phone number of my cleaning lady. She was still there when I came home and finished up while I was sleeping."

"You have a cleaning lady?"

"What's wrong with that? A lot of single guys—"

"Gotta go," she suddenly hissed, cutting him off midsentence. "Mary Holland Park, Saturday at one." And the line clicked dead.

For several moments, he stared at his open phone, as if searching for answers hidden in the image on its glowing screen. Why did Melissa and BethAnn both assume he was with someone else? And what did Mary Holland Park have to do with anything? He had heard of it, but had no idea where it was.

He snapped the phone shut and strolled to his room. Tomorrow he would do an internet search for Mary Holland Park. And Saturday he would be there…at one.

Because whatever was significant about Mary Holland Park, he was sure it had something to do with Missy.

And everything to do with his attempts to win her back.

# ELEVEN

Melissa's eyes shot open, and she lay motionless in the darkness. Everything was deathly still. There was no wind, no scrape of branches against the roof, no approaching storm with its eerie light display and ominous rumble.

But something jarred her out of a sound sleep.

For several moments she waited, listening, eyes wide, every muscle taut. A creak broke the silence, sending shock waves ricocheting through her body. She drew in a shaky breath. If she didn't stop waking with every creak and groan of the old house, she was going to lose her mind.

She rolled onto her side, dragging the spare pillow with her and clutching it to her chest. The alarm clock announced she had once again awoken in the dead of night, its red numerals glowing eerily in the darkness. Except it wasn't totally dark. Not as usual. A faint glow emanated from the open door.

Goose bumps cascaded over her, and her heart began to pound. Was she simply seeing the light that found its way inside from the front porch and patio out back? Or was it coming from somewhere inside the house?

She lay unmoving, listening, staring through the doorway and into the hall. This time there were no apparitions. And all was quiet except the occasional creaks that were as much a part of the old house as the plumbing. She would never get used to them, but maybe eventually they wouldn't set her teeth on edge.

She slid from the bed and tiptoed into the hall. The source of the light was definitely inside. For several long moments she waited at the top of the stairs, longing to run back to her room, lock the door and call the police. But she had already made that mistake once.

She probably left the light on herself. It was late when she got home from BethAnn's, and she was tired. She was also distracted. More than likely, she plodded up the stairs and fell into bed, not giving the lights a second thought.

Decision made, she began her descent, carefully avoiding the steps that creaked. Her heart pounded in her chest, and she reached the bottom feeling like the stupid heroine Chris joked about, investigating the bump in the night instead of calling the police.

But this was different. Aside from the usual creaks, there were no bumps. And the light being on had a logical explanation. Especially with the dead bolt in the locked position.

The moment she stepped into the kitchen, her breath caught in her throat. One of the chairs was angled away from the table. An icy chill settled over her, and she hugged her arms to her chest. She may have turned on the light, but she hadn't sat at the table. She had eaten at BethAnn's—leftover roast while they watched the movie.

But the back door was still locked. So was the door going into the garage. She crossed the kitchen and put her hands on the chair. A chill passed over her again, raising the hair on the back of her neck. It was as if someone had been there, touched the chair and left behind remnants of something unsettling. She shot an uneasy glance over her shoulder and slid the chair into place. No one had come into the house. She was just on edge.

Granted, she was being stalked. Someone was watching her come and go, even looking in the windows. But he couldn't pass through walls. So that left one explanation.

She had turned on the light and moved the chair herself.

She flipped the switch and trudged back up the stairs. Daylight was still two hours away, and she needed sleep. She had a lot of work to do—a full day of depositions at the state attorney's office.

Then tonight she would call Chris.

He had called three times and left one message, which she deleted without playing back. Then she turned her phone off.

But she couldn't avoid him forever. She was going to have to face him, if not in person, at least over the phone. *Preferably* over the phone. Then she wouldn't be swayed by that warm gaze and teasing smile. She could tune out the smooth timbre of his voice and focus on the words—whatever cockamamie explanation he might come up with for why a woman answered his phone.

Then she would tell him not to call her anymore. She didn't need his protection. If things got too scary and she didn't feel the Harmony Grove Police Department could handle it, she would run. She had done it before; she could do it again.

And she didn't want a relationship, or even friendship. She wanted a clean and final break. Then she could move forward. Actually, she would be happy to move back—one month ago, she was quite content with her life and how neatly she had stuffed Chris and all related memories into some dusty, cobwebbed corner of her mind.

Somehow she would get there again.

Chris picked up his phone from the end table and sank into his dad's recliner. After all the calls Missy had ignored last night, he didn't expect tonight to be any different. But he had to give it a try. He waited through several rings, silently willing her to answer. When her message came on, her voice, pure and sweet, wound its way right into his heart, and he closed his eyes against the sense of loss sweeping over him. He couldn't have blown it that badly. It was such a minor mess-up. She had to see that eventually.

He left a message, much the same as the one he left

the prior night. Now he would have to wait till Saturday. Maybe by then she would be willing to listen.

He picked up the remote and pressed the power button. Canned laughter filled the living room, the product of some senseless evening sitcom. But his mind wasn't on the characters and their issues—he had enough issues of his own.

Three more vendors had cut him off, and now that all the checks had cleared, he wouldn't have enough funds to make payroll this week without wiping out the last of his personal savings account. Donna had seen to that, with two final four-thousand-dollar checks to her phony company two days before she disappeared. But the worst blow came when Karen called about the mortgage. Donna had made interest-only payments for the past five years, and the full amount was coming due in four months.

He picked up the remote and advanced the channel. The canned laughter was getting on his nerves. So were the off-color jokes that really weren't funny. The scene switched from a New York City lounge to the Serengeti Plains. A cheetah stalked a herd of gazelles, pacing back and forth, eyeing one unfortunate female lagging behind.

He laid the remote on the table and settled back in his recliner. The cheetah's escapades would be far more engaging than Tom's bumbling attempts at finding George a date. And that soon-to-be-devoured gazelle—he could relate. He would never dig himself out of the mess he was in. The only option left was for the store to file bankruptcy.

When his phone rang moments later, he snatched it up, hoping but not really expecting it to be Melissa. He was pleasantly surprised. Elated, actually. He flipped it open so quickly that the ringtone didn't even reach full volume. She would think he was holding the phone, pining away, waiting for her to call. He didn't care.

"I'm glad you called me back." He rushed ahead, making sure he got his chance to explain before she shot him down. "I'm sorry about last night. I had a massive headache when I got home, took some pain-killers and lay down, never intending to fall asleep. Well, the next thing I knew, it was eight o'clock."

She responded with a disgusted sigh. "Don't insult me by lying to me. She answered your phone. You've been caught. Again."

Her reminder of the past was a well-aimed barb, an arrow piercing his heart. It sank deep, its poison of guilt and regret spreading throughout his body and seeping into his bones. He had already explained everything to her, why he had made his accusations, why he didn't trust her. And he assured her that nothing happened between him and Adrianne. Didn't she believe him?

She obviously didn't believe him now. "My phone never rang." Of course, it was in the kitchen, and he was dead to the world. But no one would have answered it. Unless… "Betty! You called and Betty answered my phone."

Realization slammed into him. No wonder Missy thought he was with another woman. The whole situation would be funny if she wasn't so mad at him. "Betty was my dad's cleaning lady. When I got home, she was still working. She must have picked up my phone when it rang."

A long, heavy silence followed, so long he was afraid his phone had dropped the call. "Missy? Are you there?"

A sigh told him she was.

"That was only Betty," he continued. "Trust me when I say there's no one else. There never has been. You're all I've ever wanted."

Another sigh came through the phone. "I'm sorry. This whole thing was a bad idea."

"What thing?"

"You and me, trying to resurrect what we had."

Was she serious? She couldn't really be thinking of giving up already. "Missy, I'm sorry. It was an accident. We can reschedule. And I promise I won't lie down, even for a minute."

"No, Chris, I just can't do it."

"What can't you do?"

"See you, be with you." Her voice caught. "I have to go."

"No, Missy, don't give up on us."

She continued as if he hadn't spoken. "Please don't call me anymore."

"Missy, wait."

And then she was gone. For several moments, he stared at the phone in dumb silence. It was over. She wasn't even going to give him a chance. All because he slept through their date. But for her, it went much deeper than that, touching a nerve that had been exposed with her father's betrayal long ago. And each of his own mistakes only reopened those wounds. He had unwittingly hurt her in the worst way possible.

He lifted his eyes to the forgotten screen. The cheetah had taken down its prey and was enjoying a good meal. The herd had moved on, unperturbed by the fate of the laggard. And that was life. Tragedies happen and people get hurt, and for the rest of the world, life continues without a hitch.

In a little over twenty-four hours, everything dear to him had slipped through his grasp. The store was teetering on the edge of bankruptcy, and the only woman he would ever love had walked out of his life forever. What was God trying to do to him?

As soon as the thought slipped into his mind, he kicked it aside. He wasn't important enough in the whole scheme of things to be singled out by God, for good or bad. Besides, if he didn't credit God for the good things, he couldn't blame Him for the bad. He hated double standards. No, God had nothing to do with the mess he was in.

He pushed the power button on the remote, plunging the Serengeti Plains into darkness. He needed some fresh air. A good run would help clear the cobwebs from his mind and give him a new perspective.

As he stepped out the door and jogged toward the sidewalk that bordered his yard, a gentle breeze rustled the trees. Fall was his favorite time of year, when cooler evenings provided some relief from the blistering days of summer and the air began to lose some of its oppressive stickiness.

But it was going to take a lot more than a sprint around the block to fix everything wrong in his life. He was at the end of his rope. And it was fraying. Some long-ago words drifted into his mind, spoken to him during the other dark time in his life. *When you reach the bottom, there's nowhere to look but up.* "Up" for his friend was God, and he was quick to say so.

God. That was the second time God had crossed his mind. Was it more than coincidence? Was God trying to get his attention?

No, that was ridiculous. God wasn't aware of him and his problems, not with billions of other people vying for His attention. In a world where every minute children are kidnapped, women raped and men murdered for no greater crime than being who they are, his problems were pretty insignificant.

But that wasn't what Missy believed. Missy believed that God was concerned with everyone, with every problem, no matter how minor. How did she put it? "God cares about every aspect of our lives."

Was it true? Did God really care about him, one small speck in a world of hurting people?

He slowed to a fast walk and lifted his gaze skyward. The moon shone brightly, a swollen crescent. Thousands of points of light hung scattered across a backdrop of inky-black. Tens of thousands more cast their light earthward, too distant to be seen with the naked eye.

God was up there somewhere. When He looked down from his throne in the sky, what did He see? A giant orb with its irregular patterns of land and sea, hanging in cold, dark space? Or could He actually see each person and know his thoughts every moment of every day? Did He even want to?

*God, are You there? Are You listening?*

There was no answer. Of course, he didn't expect one. That wasn't how God worked. Not that he had any firsthand knowledge. Actually, when it came to communicating with God, he had all the wisdom and understanding of a box of rocks. He began again.

*God, if You help me save the store and get Missy back…* He cut off the thought midsentence. No, those get-me-out-of-this-mess-and-I'll-serve-you-forever kind of prayers reeked of hypocrisy. If he was going to make a commitment, it was going to be a heartfelt one with no strings attached.

*God,* he began once more, *I don't even know how to do this. Help me know You're there. I want to give my life to You. I don't know if You even want it, be-*

*cause right now it's a pretty big mess. But I need Your help. I can't do this alone.*

He once again broke into a full run, sneakered feet pounding the sidewalk as energy surged through him. His faltering prayer had been heard. Somehow he knew. He couldn't explain it if he had to. There were no lightning bolts, no voices from heaven.

Just an overwhelming sense of peace—not that everything was going to be all right, but that whatever happened, he wouldn't be alone.

# TWELVE

"There's got to be a way to hit the triple word score, but I sure can't see it." Mrs. Johnson laid down her tiles, ending one space shy of a red square.

Melissa frowned at the board. "I had a way, which you've ruined, incidentally."

"Sorry about that." She wasn't, really. Mrs. Johnson took her games seriously and didn't cut anyone any slack.

Two soft knocks sounded on the front door, followed by creaking hinges.

"Grandma?"

"In the kitchen."

Moments later, Dennis's stocky frame filled the doorway. His eyes registered surprise when he saw her sitting there with his grandmother. Of course, he probably already knew. He was likely watching her from the moment she stepped through the gate until she disappeared into the house.

"Help yourself." Mrs. Johnson picked up a plate filled with thick slices of banana-nut bread and set it on the edge of the table. "I told Dennis to come and get some when it came out of the oven. He loves my banana-nut bread."

Melissa smiled at her elderly neighbor. "Dennis and half the world." Even if she wasn't such a game buff, she would probably still agree to monthly game night just for Mrs. Johnson's banana-nut bread.

Throughout the next round, Dennis silently munched his bread and watched them play. His gaze on her at close range was a little less disturbing than his presence at the apartment window. Maybe it was because his grandmother sat right across the table. Or maybe his observing their game just wasn't as creepy as the way he sat hour after hour holed up in that apartment, keeping his silent vigil.

Mrs. Johnson laid some tiles on the tray and sighed. "Melissa's beating me tonight. That seven-letter word she played pretty much did me in. But I'll get her next time."

Dennis grunted a response and stuffed the remaining half slice into his mouth. Then he retraced his path to the front door, his gait an irreverent strut-shuffle that announced his general annoyance with life.

After the front door creaked shut, Mrs. Johnson leaned forward, voice lowered. "I finally kicked him out. He's got till tomorrow. I can't keep supporting him while he plays video games and draws all day. He's got talent. But he needs to do something with it." She shook her head and frowned. "I hate to be the one to teach it, but he's got to learn some responsibility."

Melissa flashed her a sympathetic smile. "I know. That's tough love, and it's never easy." Especially for a kind soul like Mrs. Johnson. She couldn't even turn away an abandoned animal, as two highly spoiled dogs and six or eight cats could attest.

"I appreciate you coming over here to play with me. Harold and I always played games after dinner." She released a long, wistful sigh. "It's been four years, and I miss him like it was yesterday. We had fifty-three wonderful years together."

Her pale blue eyes grew soft with love and cherished memories. And it stirred something in Melissa, a longing for a life that seemed completely out of reach. "You're blessed. A lot of women would kill for a taste of what you had. Especially nowadays. They just don't make men like that anymore."

Mrs. Johnson took a sip of her tea and placed the china cup back on the saucer. "There are still good men out there. You just have to know how to recognize them."

Yeah, and how many mistakes would it take to learn? She didn't exactly trust her instincts when it came to spotting good men. One bad choice after another worked for her mother, but not for her.

Mrs. Johnson drew the last three tiles from the box. "Well, I'd say you've got me for sure. Unless 'wbshitz' is a word and there's a place to play it, I don't stand a chance."

Melissa made the last play and finished thirty-four points in the lead. But Mrs. Johnson was right—she probably *would* get her next time. After sixty-plus years of playing, the old woman had half the Scrabble dictionary memorized.

Mrs. Johnson followed her through the foyer and onto the porch. "Are you comfortable walking home alone?"

"I think I'll be okay." She shot a glance toward the garage apartment. For once, Dennis wasn't watching her. In fact, even though the light was on inside, his form wasn't at either of the windows. That wasn't exactly reassuring. If he wasn't in the apartment, where was he?

"I'll watch you from here."

She nodded and started down the walk. She had decided not to go out alone at night anymore. But this was different. Number one, it was right next door; hopefully she could slip out and back unobserved. Number two, Mrs. Johnson really looked forward to their game nights, and she hated to disappoint her.

But next time she would bring a flashlight.

She stepped from the end of the walk and waited for her eyes to adjust. The glow from Mrs. Johnson's porch light stopped at the driveway, and the spotlight on the front of the garage was out. She started across the yard, feeling her way toward the fence. The half-moon peeking through the edge of the clouds wasn't much help. Neither were the few stars whose light managed to escape through holes in the puffy charcoal blanket.

By the time she reached the gate, she was kicking

herself for deciding to walk home in the dark. She could have asked Dennis to accompany her. But that option wasn't any more comforting than the thought of walking home alone. And it seemed silly to have Mrs. Johnson drive her when she lived right next door.

She found the gate and cast a glance back at the house. Mrs. Johnson still waited on the porch, soft light falling all around her. But her own form wouldn't be visible. From Mrs. Johnson's perspective, darkness had swallowed her the moment she stepped past the garage, darkness that also lay thick and heavy in front of her. Uneasiness sifted over her, and she clutched her key more tightly.

When she turned to close the gate, her heart leaped into her throat and lodged there. Not four feet away stood a figure, a vague silhouette against the faint glow of the porch light. A scream rose in her throat, and she threw up both hands as if to defend herself.

"Whoa, lady."

The voice belonged to Dennis, but that wasn't any consolation. The threat didn't lessen; it just moved from unknown to known. She sucked in a steadying breath and tried to still her pounding heart. He had emerged from his cave for a reason, and the sooner she found out what it was, the better. "Can I help you?"

"Actually, you can."

He stepped through the opening and closed the gate. The simple motion sent panic coursing through her. She looked past him to see Mrs. Johnson turn and step back into the house, taking away her last thread of security. What did Dennis want with her?

Now that her eyes had adjusted to the darkness, he was no longer just a vague shape. He cleared his throat and shifted his weight from one foot to the other. He actually seemed unsure of himself, that ever-present chip on his shoulder gone, or at least much smaller.

"My grandmother's kicking me out," he began, "and I need a place to stay. Can I rent a room from you?"

Her jaw dropped. It was bad enough having him watch her from the garage apartment next door. But having him inside the house? Even if he didn't give her the creeps, she didn't need a mooch taking up residence in one of her bedrooms. "I can't rent you a room. It's not my house."

"Why not? It's plenty big enough. And you wouldn't have to tell the Tylers."

"No!" she exclaimed, the last of her fear giving way to indignation. "I'm not going to do something behind their back."

He shifted his weight again. "What about the stable? The Tylers wouldn't care if I stayed out there."

She heaved an exasperated sigh. "I'm going to tell you the same thing I told someone else recently. It's not livable. It doesn't lock, it leaks and it's ready to fall down."

"Please. I'm not picky." He dropped his hand from the gate and stepped closer.

She held her ground. "The Tylers won't let you stay there. It would be a liability."

He gave it one last-ditch effort. "My parents don't want me. I don't have anywhere to go."

"I'm sorry."

He flipped up the latch on the gate, the movement fast and sharp. The chip was back. And it had gained some mass during its brief absence. He wasn't just annoyed. He was mad.

"You're just like my family," he spat. "Greedy, stingy and won't share with anyone else."

He shoved the gate open with enough force that it swung back and hit the fence with a solid clang. Then he stalked toward his temporary home, kicking at the ground as he went.

And she strode toward her own temporary home, thankful that by tomorrow evening, they would no longer be neighbors. Now that he was so angry with her, she wasn't going to rest easy until he was gone.

Chris tore his gaze from the pavilion in the distance and returned his attention to the scene around him. The picket-fenced area where he sat was a flurry of activity. Children played on a huge jungle gym, swarming over its surface like multicolored ants. Others sailed one by one down a tall metal slide and circled around to do it all over again. Every swing was occupied, their offbeat rhythm of squeaks punctuating the symphony of happy voices. The carefree scene provided a welcome distraction.

Nothing in his life had improved. He had talked to the bank about his situation, hoping to get the mortgage renewed, or at least extended, but it didn't look very promising. Both Sam and Derrick had said they would hang in there as long as they could. But if something more secure opened up for either of them, they would have to take it. Karen didn't make any promises one way or the other.

And nothing had changed with Missy. He hadn't talked to her since Tuesday night. But not an hour had passed that he didn't worry about her. She needed protection—protection that Alan was too inexperienced to give. And Branch just didn't care. So he had enlisted Ron's aid once again. If he could just track down this Eugene creep, he would feel so much better. Missy didn't believe Eugene had found her, but he wasn't so sure.

His attention slid back over to the pavilion. Missy sat at the concrete table underneath, along with Kevin and BethAnn. He had seen them arrive, watched while they toted picnic supplies from BethAnn's van. But he hadn't approached them. And frankly, he didn't know how. Since he arrived at twelve-thirty, he had been racking his brain for a way to keep her guard from going up instantly. At least when he showed up at the mall, he had an excuse.

But when the three of them had finished lunch and headed in his direction, the decision was made for him. BethAnn spotted him, and a wide smile spread across her face.

"Hey, Chris," she shouted, waving enthusiastically.

Melissa's reaction wasn't so welcoming. Her eyes narrowed, and she crossed her arms stubbornly in front of her. He stood to go meet them.

"It's good to see you again," BethAnn exclaimed. "What are you doing here?"

*God bless BethAnn.* She was a good one to have in his corner. "Doing some people watching. It's too nice of a day to spend inside."

"Yeah, right," Melissa said, sarcasm heavy in her tone. "Your showing up here is as much a coincidence as your showing up at the mall." She turned an accusing stare on BethAnn. "You called him, didn't you? You told him I was going to be here today."

"No, I didn't call him."

"Okay, you went by the store."

BethAnn was doing her best to stifle a grin. "No, I didn't go by the store, either."

Melissa planted both hands firmly on her hips, but she didn't look nearly as annoyed as he expected. Maybe BethAnn had been working on her. "Okay, you talked to him, left him a note, wired a telegram, sent up smoke signals—somehow you let him know I was going to be here today."

"You caught me." She released the grin she had tried to restrain. "He called your phone while you were in the bathroom, and I answered. But it was up to him whether he wanted to come. I'd say he really wanted to see you."

That was an understatement. He had hardly thought of anything else all week.

"But since he's here, what do you say he tags along?" BethAnn turned to look at him. "We're headed to the fort."

"The fort?" He had scanned the park when he arrived. A narrow asphalt road wound through, offering easy access to about a dozen pavilions. In the distance, two small bridges spanned a thin ribbon of water that connected two lakes. The playground was at the other end. Beyond it were soccer fields. Nothing he had seen resembled a fort.

"Well, it's not really a fort," BethAnn admitted. "It's actually a big mound of dirt with two short concrete block walls going up one side and down the other. It was my favorite spot in the whole world when I was eight. All us kids played make-believe there." Her eyes sparkled with fond memories. "I was a princess being held captive in a wicked king's castle. Then the brave knights would come charging up with their sticks and rescue me."

"Sounds like fun," Melissa said. "I just want to know how come I missed out on this place."

"I'm not sure. It's just a twenty-minute drive, but the only times I came were when I spent the weekend with my aunt and uncle over here. My cousins and I would play for hours. We were all sure the fort was enchanted."

When BethAnn reached the edge of the soccer field, she stopped suddenly, brows drawn together in confusion. "I can't believe it. The fort's gone. They took my mound."

Kevin shook his head and made a clucking sound. "Those dirty, low-down mound thieves."

"I'm serious," BethAnn protested. "It was right here. I'm positive."

"Sure it was." Kevin's tone was patronizing.

BethAnn put her hands on her hips. "I'll prove it to you." She stalked over to where a small group of men and women were forming teams for a volleyball game. "Do you know what happened to the old fort that used to be here?"

Several shook their heads. Finally a woman stepped forward. "Yeah, they tore it down several years back to put in the soccer field."

BethAnn turned defiantly to Kevin. "See, I told you I wasn't nuts."

Kevin grinned. "Yeah, you are, but that's beside the point."

She playfully punched him in the stomach, and he grabbed both her wrists. Somewhere near five foot nine, he wasn't much taller than BethAnn. He looked like a surfer, with skin bronzed golden-brown and sun-bleached hair that he was constantly pushing out of his eyes. But according to Missy, that killer tan came from hours spent working his landscape-design business rather than riding the waves.

Kevin released her hands to pull her into an embrace that was half restraint, half affection. As Chris watched, a sense of nostalgia crept up on him. It seemed to hit him at odd times, triggered by seemingly innocent events. There were a lot of things he missed about his relationship with Missy. Playfulness was one of them.

BethAnn and Kevin's horseplay was interrupted by one of the team members. "Hey, would y'all want to join us? We're short."

Chris opened his mouth to decline. This was his chance to talk to Missy, and he wasn't going to waste it.

But BethAnn spoke first. "You guys go ahead. Melissa and I will watch."

Kevin slapped him roughly on the back, and Beth-Ann led Missy away, throwing a monkey wrench into all his plans. But BethAnn evidently had plans of her own. As the game progressed, he repeatedly caught them watching him, engrossed in heavy conversation. The instant he and Kevin approached, their words died.

Kevin held out a hand to pull BethAnn to her feet. "You guys don't make very good cheerleaders. You were supposed to be rooting for our team and praising all our brilliant shots. Instead you were yakking the whole time. But we still won two out of three without our cheering section."

BethAnn smiled up at him. "We'll try to be a little more attentive next time."

Chris watched her slip an arm around Kevin's

waist and snuggle into his side. Missy had let him help her up but had pulled her hand free as soon as she was on her feet. And although she walked next to him, it was with that familiar closed stance, arms crossed in front of her. This was his chance to talk to her, but he had no idea where to begin.

He flashed her a weak smile. "I hope you're not too upset at me for crashing your picnic. I really wanted to see you."

She shrugged but didn't respond. She wasn't making it easy for him.

"Has anyone bothered you since I last talked to you?"

"No, it's been pretty quiet."

"Good." He stuffed his hands into his pockets, not sure what to say next. They had reached the picnic area and were heading toward one of the lakes. Kevin and BethAnn walked hand in hand some ten or fifteen feet in front of them. Missy didn't look any more relaxed than when they had started.

"Well, I wanted to let you know I called my partner. I don't want to keep anything from you."

She dropped her arms to let them swing at her sides, something he took as a good sign. "And?"

"He's doing searches, seeing if Eugene's name shows up. If the creep was seen anywhere near here, I'd like to know it."

"So would I."

They stepped onto one of the two bridges that spanned the narrow canal, but instead of following BethAnn and Kevin, Melissa stopped halfway across to stand at the wooden rail. Lilies and hyacinths formed a floor far below, the shallow water hidden somewhere beneath. Towering cypress trees rose from the depths, draped in Spanish moss. The whole scene was Florida at its purest.

But Missy didn't seem to be taking in the scenery. Her gaze was distant, fixed on some point where the canal met the lake. What was she thinking about? Once upon a time, he would have just asked.

"Missy, you know how I feel about you. Let me be there for you."

She shook her head, her hands gripping the rail until her knuckles turned white.

"I'm not like your father, Missy. Give me a chance to prove it to you."

"I can't. Not yet." She turned to look up at him, her eyes moist. "This isn't goodbye. It's just… I need some space. I have a lot of things to work through, and I can't do that with you calling and dropping by all the time."

He nodded slowly. That wasn't exactly what he wanted to hear. But it was a far cry from what she'd told him Tuesday night. BethAnn must have presented some pretty persuasive arguments. He would thank her later.

But he didn't just have BethAnn to thank. Over the past four days, he had sent up a lot of prayers. They had evidently been heard.

*Thank You, God.*

# THIRTEEN

"You're quiet." BethAnn turned around in the seat to look back at Melissa.

Of course she was quiet. Just four days ago she had it all figured out. Now, thanks to BethAnn's hour-long pep talk, she was facing decisions that could affect the rest of her life.

"I'm just thinking."

"No, you're *over*thinking. You need to jump in and give Chris a chance. You've prayed about it, but God can't guide your path if you refuse to take the first step."

"That's easy for you to say. You've already got your Mr. Right."

"And you very well might have yours. But you'll never know if you keep yourself locked away, scared to death you're going to get hurt."

BethAnn had a point. Of course, trust came easy for BethAnn. She hadn't had hers shattered so many times. "If it'll make you feel any better, I didn't give him a yes, but I didn't give him a no, either. I left him with a definite maybe."

"I guess that's a start."

Kevin eased to a stop in the gravel drive, and BethAnn again turned in her seat. "We'll watch and make sure you get inside okay. And if you need us for anything, give us a call. I don't care what time it is."

"Thanks, I appreciate it." She started up the front walk, empty potato-salad bowl in hand, and suddenly froze. Another envelope was taped to the front door. She spun back around, but BethAnn was already climbing from the van, face creased in concern. "It's another note, isn't it?"

By the time she removed it from the door, both Kevin and BethAnn had joined her. But that didn't stop the chill from sweeping over her, or quiet her tumbling thoughts as she read.

*Melissa, I never considered the possibility that there might be someone else. Watching him come and go is driving an arrow ever deeper into my heart. You know who I mean. Every time I see him with you, I can hardly refrain from taking matters into my own hands.*

*But the predestined time has not arrived. When it does, I will prove my worthiness. I will climb the highest mountain, cross the deepest sea, rehang the moon and the stars. Then you will understand the strength of my love for you. You are a prize worth fighting for.*

She closed her eyes, and a shudder shook her shoulders. The chill sank deeper into her bones, penetrating all the way to her soul. Who was stalking her? This wasn't penned by an angry young man like Dennis. And it didn't fit with what she knew of Eugene, at least not the Eugene who had pinned her against the wall with a knife at her throat. That Eugene had no words of adoration. Only threats.

"He's getting weirder and weirder," BethAnn whispered, "totally losing touch with reality."

"And he's threatening Chris," Melissa added. "All the more reason for him to stay away."

BethAnn gave her a wry smile. "Somehow I can't imagine that deterring him."

"I guess I need to call the police again." She sighed and refolded the note. "I always hope for Alan but usually get stuck with Branch. He looks down his nose at all us lowly civilians, but he especially dislikes me and my family."

Kevin nodded. "You know what they say about love spurned."

"What? Who?" She looked from Kevin to Beth-Ann, but BethAnn's blank stare reflected her own.

Kevin went on to explain. "After your father left, Branch kept hitting on your mother."

"He did?" She wrinkled her nose. "I remember him coming around a lot. I just thought that's what policemen do, you know, watch out for women and children who don't have a man to protect them."

BethAnn looked at her with raised eyebrows.

"Hey, I was nine," she said defensively. "So Chief Branch had the hots for my mom. That's actually kind of gross."

"Evidently your mother thought so, too. But Branch wouldn't give up. He was persistent to the point of being laughable."

BethAnn eyed Kevin suspiciously. "And you know all this how?"

"I was an incredibly mature fifth grader at the time. You two were mere babes."

BethAnn poked him in the ribs. "We're just a year younger than you."

Kevin laughed. "My older sisters used to talk about it. He made quite a fool of himself."

Melissa nodded slowly, letting the revelation sink in. "So that explains why Branch has it in for the whole Langston family."

She pulled out her cell phone and punched in Harmony Grove's nonemergency number. Maybe she would end up with Chief Branch. But now that she knew the reason behind his dislike for her, it would be much harder for him to push her buttons.

Chris looked at the number displayed on his phone, and his heart jumped to double time. Ron was calling back with the information he'd requested. "What have you got?"

"Not much. Seems the guy is lying low. But a Eugene Holmes did get stopped about four weeks ago near Lake City. Got cited for a headlamp out. He was in an '84 Chevy Malibu, which matches the description your lady gave in several of her reports. I'm going to call Florida and have them put out a BOLO, just in case he's still there. And I'll keep checking, too."

"Thanks." He changed the sign from Open to Closed and armed the store's alarm system. What was Eugene doing near Lake City? Did he have business there? Or was he headed to Harmony Grove? If so, Missy was in more imminent danger than she realized. He had to let her know. And he couldn't tell her over the phone.

Just Saturday he had promised to give her her space. Well, that was a promise he wouldn't be able to keep. Because now that Eugene had been spotted in Florida, he was afraid to let her out of his sight.

As he sped toward Harmony Grove, the sun sank lower in the sky. Was Eugene lurking somewhere nearby, waiting for darkness to make his move? *God, he prayed, I'm putting her in Your hands. Please protect her.* The worry abated for a brief moment, then slid right back in, turning his insides into a tangled mass of nerves. He was too new at this whole prayer thing.

He reached the end of her street, and the lump in his gut grew. The long gravel drive was empty. She should be home by now. It would be dark within the hour. He stepped from the truck and paced the front yard, trying to relieve the tension spiraling through him. It didn't help. Neither did calling her, because when she didn't answer, his imagination went into overdrive.

Twenty minutes passed before the crunch of gravel announced her return. She eased to a stop and stepped from the car. "What are you doing here?"

"Where have you been?" The accusatory words escaped before he could censure them, and earned him just the reaction he expected.

"Where I've been is none of your concern. I told you to give me my space." She started to brush past him, but his hand on her shoulder stopped her.

"I'm sorry. I didn't mean it like that. I thought you would be here, and when you didn't answer your phone, I feared the worst."

Her eyes flicked over him, and her features softened. "I had a deposition that ran late. Then I had to stop and pick up a few things. I guess I left my phone on vibrate." She pressed a button on her key fob, and the trunk released. "So why are you here?"

"I heard from Ron."

She spun to face him, whatever was in the trunk momentarily forgotten. "And?"

"A Eugene Holmes was stopped for a traffic violation near Lake City four weeks ago. He was driving an '84 Chevy Malibu."

The color leached from her face, and she sagged against the side of the car, clutching her stomach and shaking her head in denial. "No, he couldn't have found me. I was so careful."

The fear in those wide blue eyes snagged his heart, and he longed to just wipe it away. But he wouldn't give her false security. "It could be nothing. He may have had business there. Lake City is only four or five hours from Atlanta. But he could also be here. I didn't want to worry you, but I had to let you know."

She didn't respond, just stalked to the back of the car and raised the lid. Half a dozen plastic bags lined the trunk, a carton of milk sticking out the top of one of them. She began snatching bags, then grabbed the case that held her steno machine. As she started up the front walk, he removed the other three bags and closed the trunk.

He caught up with her in the kitchen, where she stood at the pantry putting cans on shelves. After putting the milk and other perishable items in the fridge, he joined her.

"Missy," he whispered, but she didn't respond, just reached into the bag at her feet and pulled out a box of cereal. He rested his hand lightly on her forearm and took the box from her. "I'm here for you, Missy. Let me help."

She turned slowly to face him. Tears threatened to pool on her lower lashes, but she blinked them away. She was trying so hard to be strong.

"Nobody expects you to do this alone. Please let me help."

She gave two brief nods and leaned back against the doorjamb of the pantry. "All right. Tell me what you have in mind."

"We need to come up with a game plan. He's left three notes so far, made it clear he's watching you. We need to get the police to stake the place out, catch him in the act. It shouldn't be that difficult. He's slick, but he's going to get careless eventually."

She raised her eyebrows. "Do you really think Branch will approve expending the resources over a few notes?"

"Probably not. But I bet Alan would be happy to put in some time on the side. He and I can load up on mosquito repellent and protein bars and camp out in your yard."

"Whoever's doing this is going to stay away while you guys are hanging around."

"He won't know. We'll slip in from Mrs. Johnson's and stay hidden in the shrubbery."

She seemed to be considering the idea when her eyes suddenly widened. "You can't be here. He threatened you in the last note. It wasn't overt, but BethAnn and I both took it that way."

"And you think that's going to stop me from being here to protect you? Not in this lifetime. Look, Alan and I will be armed."

"He might be, too."

"But there are two of us. And we're both trained law enforcement."

She pushed herself away from the pantry, closed the door and walked to the fridge. She didn't exactly acquiesce, but she wasn't arguing anymore. "Would you like to stay for dinner? Nothing fancy. I'm just doing chicken and yellow rice."

"I'd love to." He watched her remove a plastic bag containing two leg quarters, which she rinsed and placed in a pan. There was something intimate about standing in the kitchen with her, preparing to have a meal together. He shook the thought from his mind. That wasn't what he was here for. She was stuck with him hanging around to see to her safety. Anything beyond that, he would respect her wishes. "Can I help you cook?"

"I've got it. But if you really want to do something, you can feed Smudge."

He crossed the room, trying unsuccessfully to coax Smudge to follow. But as soon as he opened the pantry door, the big white cat was beside him.

"You *are* ready to eat. So what'll it be?" He picked up two cans. "This one, or…this one."

Smudge responded with a hearty meow.

"Okay, savory turkey and vegetables. Good choice." He bent to pick up the empty food dish and popped the top on the can. "And are you a half-can or full-can kind of kitty?"

"Half can," Missy answered, in chorus with another meow from Smudge.

"No, Mommy says half can, and we have to do what she says." He put the dish on the floor, and the cat dug in amid satisfied smacks and purrs.

When he straightened back up, Missy eyed him with an amused smile.

"What?"

"I was just listening to your conversation with my deaf cat."

"Well, he answered every question I asked."

"No," she argued, "he was protesting because you didn't get his food down fast enough."

He leaned back against the cabinet. The chicken had begun to boil, and an unopened package of rice lay on the counter. "So where's the smudge? I haven't seen it."

"He doesn't have one. When he was a kitten, he had two on top of his head, but they disappeared as he got older."

"So now you have a solid white cat named Smudge."

"Yep." She grinned up at him. "By the time the smudges disappeared, it was too late to change his name. Not that he minded." She opened the fridge and straightened with several kinds of salad ingredients in her arms.

While she finished dinner, he retrieved Alan's number from her phone and proceeded to lay out his plans. Alan was totally on board, eager to assist in any way he could.

"Well, it's set." He pocketed his phone. "Tomorrow night we'll show up shortly after dark. Alan's off Wednesday, so he doesn't mind staying up all night."

She placed a steaming bowl of chicken and rice between the two place settings already on the table. "And what about you? You're not off Wednesday."

"I'll grab some sleep in the morning and go in

late." He sat at one of the places in the little nook, and she took the chair opposite him. And he was once again struck with that same sense of intimacy he'd felt watching her cook. At one time, they had been so close to a lifetime of meals just like this one. Then it was gone, all his dreams up in smoke, and he was left holding the ashes of a tomorrow that would never be.

"I was planning to watch a movie tonight."

Her words cut into his thoughts, which was good. Because his mind had started down a path it had no business being on. "What are you going to watch?"

"I don't remember the name. It's a romantic comedy I just got in the mail. Would you like to join me?" She seemed hesitant to see him go. He really couldn't blame her.

He flashed her a crooked smile. "You're going to make me sit through a chick flick, aren't you?"

"It's not *that* chick flick-ish. So it shouldn't compromise your masculinity too much."

He didn't care. He would watch *Steel Magnolias* with her if it would take that haunted look from her eyes.

By the time she walked him to the door, it was almost nine o'clock. He turned to face her in the foyer. "Thanks for dinner. And the movie. I enjoyed it."

She grinned up at him. "Even though there weren't any car chases or dead bodies?"

"Even without the car chases and dead bodies."

"Well, thanks for taking care of Smudge. I'm sure he appreciated it."

"It was my pleasure. He's a good conversationalist."

She continued to look up at him, lips parted. And all he could think about was how badly he wanted to kiss her. The scent of her perfume, probably applied early that morning, was almost gone now, shadowed remnants of citrus and spice that whispered past the edges of his consciousness, tantalizingly out of reach.

He mentally shook himself. He was here to protect her. Nothing else. "I would say see you tomorrow night, but you won't see us. We'll be there, though."

"Good. You don't know how reassuring that is." She smiled again, appreciation shining from her eyes.

He needed to leave—step back, walk out the door and drive away. But his body wouldn't obey his brain's commands. Something held him rooted to the spot, and he knew exactly what it was. It was that vulnerability that she always kept hidden except in moments like these, when the facade of strength and stubbornness fell away.

Then she moistened her lips, and that was all it took. He leaned forward slowly, and her eyes fluttered closed. When his lips met hers, the shock went all the way to his toes. Warmth flooded him—tenderness and total contentment. This was where he belonged.

Her arms sliding around his neck had all the effect of a dousing with cold water. Kissing her like this was wrong. She was afraid and vulnerable, and he was taking advantage of the whole situation.

He backed away, letting her arms fall from his neck. "I'm sorry. I promised I'd give you your space and not put any pressure on you. And I'm going to do my best to keep that promise. When and if we move beyond where we are right now, it's going to be in your time, not mine. The next kiss, if there is one, will be initiated by you. I love you too much to push you into something you're not ready for."

Her gaze fluttered to the floor, and she shifted her weight uncomfortably from one foot to the other. Was it the admission of his love that had shaken her, or his kiss? He mentally kicked himself. If he didn't rein in what he felt, he was going to push her away.

He reached up to cup her cheek. "Be careful. And wish us luck tomorrow night."

She lifted her eyes to meet his and drew in a steadying breath. "I'll do better than that. I'll pray for you."

He pulled out of the driveway, worry coiling deep in his gut. He was leaving her completely unprotected. But what else could he do? She wouldn't let him move into the house, and she insisted the stable was uninhabitable. If only her neighbors lived closer.

His gaze followed his thoughts, roaming in the direction of old Mrs. Johnson's place. At the edge of the road, illuminated in the beams of his headlights, was a sign: For Rent, Garage Apartment. He jammed on the brakes, heart singing.

He couldn't have come up with a more perfect solution if he had orchestrated it himself.

* * *

Melissa padded up the stairs, feeling more confused than ever. Why did she let him kiss her? That would only give him false hope, silent promises she had no idea if she could even keep. But she still had feelings for him, feelings that had only grown stronger since she learned the truth of what had happened five years earlier. And that was why she had let him kiss her. Her hesitancy to let down her guard and trust him didn't do anything to lessen what she felt for him.

With a sigh, she stepped into her room. Smudge bounded past her. It was bedtime—his favorite time of day, next to meal time. Actually, it was one of hers, too, when she would sit propped up against several pillows, a good book in her hand and a warm, purring body against her hip. That thirty minutes was her brief respite, her escape from the uneasiness that always wrapped around her as darkness blanketed the house.

A few days ago, she'd started sleeping with a nightlight, something she had never done in her life. It hadn't helped. And yesterday she bought a second litter box and set it up in the bathroom so she could close and lock the bedroom door. That made her feel a little more secure. Of course, an interior lock could easily be picked with nothing more high-tech than a bobby pin.

When she emerged from the bathroom, face washed and teeth brushed, Smudge was already stretched out on the bed. She pulled her nightgown from the drawer, but before she could shed her clothes, the ringing of the doorbell jarred the silence. Her blood turned to ice in her veins. Who would be ringing her bell at almost nine-thirty at night?

The moment the lingering tone of the bell faded to silence, seven raps followed, a familiar rhythm that she would never forget as long as she lived. It was their special code, a knock as personalized as a desk name plate. She hurried down the stairs and, as a final precaution before opening the door, checked the peephole. As expected, it was Chris.

He flashed her a crooked smile. "I came back for another kiss."

Before she could respond, his expression grew serious, and he brought his hand out from behind his back. In it was an envelope. He held it as if it was something too vile to touch, his middle finger against the top edge and his thumb against the bottom.

"This was on your door when I came back. I checked all around your yard, but he was gone. He probably hightailed it out of here the instant I pulled in the drive."

"What does it say?"

"I haven't opened it. We need to turn it over to the police."

"I have to know what it says."

He raised his brows at the urgency in her tone. But she had to know. If anything happened to him while he was trying to protect her, she would never forgive herself.

He hesitated for several moments, indecision in his eyes. Finally, he shook the contents of the envelope onto the Bombay chest and carefully unfolded the single sheet, touching only its edges. That was why he had held the envelope the way he had. He was trying to preserve any fingerprints left behind. She had handled each of the prior three notes, never once thinking about prints. Of course, that was his job.

She stepped up beside him to read the page now spread out on the chest.

*Melissa, I see he is still coming around. He was here when you came home, and he stayed all evening. It's not right. I am the chosen one but must love you from afar while he is loving you openly. You need to make him leave. Fate will not allow any interference. If he continues, it won't be pleasant for him. You better heed my warning.*

*As for me, this is but a test, one of many obstacles I must overcome. But I will triumph. Whatever test is put before me, I will succeed. Our time is coming. And when it does, I will take you away. You will be mine forever.*

She lifted her eyes from the page, panic pounding up her spine. Each note was getting more bizarre than the last, a written record of a headlong plunge into insanity. "You can't keep coming around," she insisted, no longer concerned for her own safety. "He's threatening you."

He shook his head. "I already told you, he's not keeping me away."

"Chris, please. I'm worried about you. If you get hurt, I'll never forgive myself."

"Look, I'm a cop. I carry a gun. I can take care of myself."

She shook her head, worry tying her stomach in knots. "I don't like it."

"I'll be careful." He reached up and cupped her cheek. "Enough of the worrisome thoughts. I came back to give you some good news. You now have a new neighbor."

She rolled her eyes. "If you're talking about the stable, no, I don't."

"I'm talking about Mrs. Johnson's garage apartment."

She stared at him for several moments, conflicting emotions tumbling through her. She was afraid for him—he wasn't staying away from danger; he was plopping himself down right in the middle of it. But she was also relieved. He was going to be next door, with an almost clear view of her bedroom window. The thought brought with it a surprising sense of security.

It would be the first good night's sleep she had had since this whole ordeal started.

# FOURTEEN

Chris sat in the straight-backed chair, shoes on and fully clothed. He wasn't comfortable. His feet were dying for a few hours of freedom after being imprisoned in tennis shoes since 7:00 a.m., and his butt and back had begun protesting hours ago.

But he wasn't looking for comfort. Comfort would only put him to sleep.

He had left Missy's at nine-thirty, fully intending to spend the night at home. But thoughts of her all alone in that huge, old house, some shadowed threat lurking just outside, chipped away at his peace of mind. By the time he reached the outskirts of Lakeland, he knew what he would do—throw the bare necessities into an overnight bag and head right back to Harmony Grove.

Now it was almost two-thirty. For three and a half hours, he had kept vigil at the apartment window, watching for any sign of movement next door. But the only prowlers he had spotted were a couple of cats and a raccoon. His post offered him a clear view of one end of the house, the same end where Missy slept. He had watched her light go out shortly after he arrived. The view of the front wasn't so clear. Two low-hanging tree limbs waved ominously back and forth, hiding, revealing, and once again hiding the walk.

He stood and stretched both arms skyward. He should probably get some sleep. Maybe he and Alan would have better luck tomorrow night. He cast one last glance through the window and stiffened, adrenaline pumping through him. Did he see something? Or was it just a shadow? He couldn't be sure because the dangling branches once again obstructed his view.

He waited for several moments, muscles taut and every sense on full alert. With the next gentle gust, he had no doubt.

Someone had just stepped onto Missy's front porch.

He flew into action, snatching up his nine millimeter from the table in front of him and dropping the spare clip into his pocket. Then he sailed down the stairs, taking them two at a time. The creep wouldn't get away this time. There would be no headlights to tip him off, nothing to warn him that he wasn't alone.

He slipped soundlessly out the back door of the garage, pistol drawn. As he made his way toward the gate separating the two yards, the rustle of branches masked his footsteps, the crunch of twigs beneath his feet something he felt more than heard. His heart pounded in anticipation. In a few short moments, it would be all over.

He slipped through the gate, and the moment he rounded the front corner of the house, he stopped dead. No one was there—not on the walk, the porch, or anywhere touched by the soft glow of the front light. If he didn't know better, he would think he imagined the shadowy figure.

But he *did* know better. Just moments earlier, someone stood on her porch. He was sure of it.

He slipped deeper into the shadows, scanning the yard for any sign of movement. The sky was clear, the moon three-quarters full. But the dense oak canopy blocked its silvery glow. And the same steady rustle that had masked his own stealthy approach was now helping his prey slip silently away.

But it didn't make sense. Not more than half a minute passed from the time he left his post at the window until he stepped into Missy's front yard. Maybe enough time for the man to move from the porch, but not enough to completely disappear from view.

It was as if he had stepped into the house.

Dread sifted over him. Surely Missy didn't leave the front door unlocked. In fact, he knew she didn't. He'd heard the dead bolt click into position before even leaving the porch. And it wasn't likely that anyone had broken in. Nothing looked damaged...at least from where he stood.

He cast another glance around the yard, then stepped from the shadows and onto the porch. The door was solid, the jamb intact. And none of the windows along the front were broken. He grasped the doorknob. As expected, it was locked.

He stepped from the porch with a discouraged sigh. He had been so close. How could the creep have eluded him so easily? Ron's words echoed in his mind: "He's apparently pretty slick because they've never caught him." Was Missy's stalker Eugene? If so, he understood why he had never been caught.

He scoured the front and then the back, knowing it was an exercise in futility but not yet ready to admit defeat and return to his room. But after a twenty-minute search of the entire yard, he had no choice. Whoever he saw was gone.

Disappeared into thin air.

Melissa pointed her toes and stretched, drawing in a full, deep breath. She'd slept better than she had in weeks. Maybe it was because she was too exhausted to do otherwise. But more likely, it was the thought that soon Chris would be right next door. He would make his move as soon as possible, maybe even later that day. The sooner, the better.

Learning Eugene had been seen in Florida knocked the foundation right out from under her. Maybe it was nothing. Maybe he'd done whatever he was doing in Lake City and had gone back to Atlanta. But there was always the possibility that he was on his way to find her. And that thought was too terrifying to face alone.

She stretched once more and rolled onto her side. Smudge was curled up on the spare pillow. For once he wasn't hiding under the bed. Evidently she wasn't the only one who felt more secure with the bedroom door closed and locked.

She glided a hand down his back several times, then climbed from the bed. It was time to get up. Multiple slashes of sunlight shone through the gaps in her miniblinds, announcing the dawn of a new day. Her first deposition wasn't until eleven, but she had transcription to do.

When she padded down the stairs, Smudge followed. He knew the routine. The first order of the day was breakfast. She stepped into the kitchen, and the next instant, strength drained from her limbs. A chair was pulled away from the table. But her gaze was locked on the envelope lying there, plain white and not addressed. It waited for her—ominous, menacing and downright terrifying. He had been in her house! No, that was impossible. Just to prove it, she checked the doors. They were locked. So where had the envelope come from?

Chris! He was there all evening. She had no idea when he'd left it, but it had to have been him. There was no other explanation.

Laughter bubbled up and overflowed, a welcome release of the tension coiled inside. Smudge waited beside his food dish, looking up at her quizzically, but he could wait. First she wanted to read Chris's note. They used to start, "Hello, beautiful," and proceed with whatever thoughts he was having at the time, romantic with an edge of silly. Or sometimes it was goofy poetry. What she wouldn't give for some of that again.

She picked up the envelope, and the last traces of tension slipped from her shoulders. There was no block print on its front, further proof that it wasn't another creepy note. It had to be from Chris. Probably words of encouragement and support that she could read and reread when he wasn't around. Smiling, she removed the contents and unfolded the single page.

The next instant, a cold blade of fear swept away all the warm, happy thoughts. Bold, black letters screamed back at her, horrifying in their familiarity. *Dear God, no! Not inside my house!*

Terror stabbed through her. It shot up her spine and lodged in her chest, squeezing the air from her lungs. Her brain shouted panicked commands. Drop the thing and run. Get away from the house and all its ghosts. But fear held her in its paralyzing grip. And though she didn't want to know what was there, her eyes roved back and forth over the words, seemingly of their own accord.

*Melissa, I love watching you sleep. Your long lashes against your cheeks, your slightly parted lips, your luscious hair flowing over your silk pillowcase. Aphrodite could not be more beautiful, or more perfect. But tonight your door is*

*closed and locked. Why are you keeping me
from your beauty?*

*Our time is growing ever closer, but it is not
yet here. I know that. The other man does not.
Someday we will face off. And I will win, because fate is on my side. I do not know what will
be required of me. If I must spill the other man's
blood to be deemed worthy, I will do it with joy,
because you are a prize worth fighting for.*

The letter slipped from her hand and fluttered to
her feet. *No!* She released the chair she held on to
for support and stumbled backward. He'd been inside the house. Touching her things. Watching her
as she slept.

Bile rose in her throat, and she clamped a hand
over her mouth. This couldn't be happening. Everything was locked. No one had come into the house.

But proof to the contrary was lying at her feet,
demanding acknowledgment. Either someone had
found a way inside, or she wrote the note herself.
Was she actually losing her mind?

She closed her eyes and hauled in a deep breath.
Nothing made sense. Her whole life felt off-kilter,
her surroundings unfamiliar. She had been picked
up and plunked down in the middle of a nightmare.

She snatched up her phone. The police were just
a call away. Let them figure it out. They would take
prints and do their investigation and maybe in the
process prove she wasn't crazy.

When she answered the door several minutes later, Chief Branch stood on her porch. Tommy Willis, the other third of the Harmony Grove police force, disappeared around the side of the house. Tommy was back from vacation. Maybe now she would see less of Branch.

She didn't mind placing her safety in Tommy's hands. In his mid-fifties, he had been a police officer for as long as she could remember and did most of his chief's legwork. He was a fixture in Harmony Grove, the one always driving around, visiting businesses, checking to see if he was needed anywhere. He would be the next chief when Branch retired, which wouldn't be anytime soon. Without his title, Branch would have to lose the conceited swagger and air of self-importance he always carried around town.

"Seeing things again?" His tone held bored indifference. He stood with his hands on his hips and back arched, putting his center of gravity over his heels. The pose made his gut even larger.

"You tell me." She handed him the note. "This was on my kitchen table this morning."

He skimmed the note, expression unreadable. "I'll take this into evidence." Then he checked the doors and windows. As before, everything was locked.

"Can you try to get prints from the table and chair?" Maybe she was grasping at straws. But there had to be something to prove she wasn't crazy, if he would just make the effort to find it.

"I'll send Tommy back in to do it," he said, and stepped out the back door.

She took a box of cereal from the pantry, then put it back. No way would she be able to eat. For the good it did her, she could have skipped the call to the police. All she had was another note to add to the ones they already had. Actually, she had two; the one from last night was still lying on the chest in the foyer. She snatched it up and headed out the front door.

When she reached the driveway, hushed male voices drifted to her from around the corner of the converted garage—Branch's slow Southern drawl, interspersed with Tommy's deep baritone.

"I don't know." The words belonged to Tommy. "That doesn't sound like Melissa."

She stopped just shy of the corner. They were talking about her!

"People do all kinds of things for attention. Besides, those Langstons—I think the whole lot of 'em are a little off. I mean, the old man dumped the lady and carried on with his girlfriend right in front of everyone, until he had the decency to move away. And look at the mother, bouncing from one man to another, gallivanting off who knows where."

Melissa's eyes widened and her jaw sagged as a wave of embarrassment washed over her. Branch was judging her for her parents' mistakes. It was so unfair! She was just about to march around the corner and tell him so when Tommy's stern tone stopped her.

"That has nothing to do with Melissa."

"Look, you haven't been here. While you were off enjoying the mountains, Alan and I were getting called out here every few days. First it was someone in her bedroom in the middle of the night. Then someone looking in the window. And all these notes, the last one left inside. But the house is always locked, and no one has a key except her and old Mrs. Johnson next door. So we have a burglar who walks through walls, watches her sleep and leaves love notes. And he never takes anything."

Tommy was silent. And she could hardly blame him. When he laid it out like that, she sounded like a total nutcase.

Branch continued. "She wants us to try to lift prints from the kitchen table and chair. So I guess we ought to appease her. Go through the motions. Just don't spend a lot of time on it."

Melissa spun around and stormed back up the sidewalk. She had heard enough. Branch was letting his prejudices stop him from doing a thorough investigation. Chris was right to be concerned about the protection she would get from Harmony Grove's finest. Branch couldn't care less about her. And Tommy and Alan couldn't go against their chief. Chris would be happy to protect her, but after the threat in the latest note, she wouldn't even consider it. Which left her one choice.

She walked through the kitchen and into the garage. The boxes from her move were still there, broken down and stored flat in the corner behind the exercise bike. She needed to get away from Harmony Grove, with its two traffic lights and intimate atmosphere. In a big city, she could disappear into the masses and stay hidden for years. She would have to give up her job. But it was a small price to pay for peace of mind. Before nightfall she would be gone.

She had just headed upstairs lugging three of the boxes and a roll of packing tape when the front door swung open.

"Melissa? Is everything okay?"

Great. It was Chris. She stopped midway up the stairs. "No, everything's not okay. I had another note this morning. This time it was on my kitchen table." She spun away to continue her ascent. By the time she reached the top, he was beside her, concern etched into his features.

"He got into your house? How?"

"I have no idea. No one has a key except Mrs. Johnson and the Tylers up in Washington. A couple weeks ago, when I was so sure I saw someone in the doorway, I called the Tylers and asked." She opened one of the boxes and drew a piece of tape across its bottom.

"What are you doing?"

"I'm leaving."

"Where are you going?"

"Somewhere big where I can get lost in the crowd and just be another nameless face." She scooped out the contents of one dresser drawer and dropped them into the box.

"Missy, give me a chance. I'm going to catch this guy."

The contents of another drawer joined the first. "I don't want your help. I don't need anybody's help." Whenever she relied on anybody else, they let her down—her dad, her mom, Chris and now the Harmony Grove police.

"You can't keep running away."

"Wanna make a bet? I did it once. I can do it again." She snatched up the roll of packing tape lying on the bed and stretched a length of it across the closed top of the box.

"Look, Missy. If you run, he'll find you. We need to end this now."

"You do what you want. I'm leaving."

"No, you're not." His eyes dropped to her purse sitting on the nightstand.

She realized his intent a moment too late. She dove for her purse just as he unclipped her keys from the D-ring on its side and dropped them into his pocket.

"Give me my keys."

"No."

She stopped her packing to glare at him. How dare he treat her like some rebellious teenager he was putting on restriction! He had definitely overstepped his bounds. "I could go downstairs right now and tell Chief Branch. He'd make you give them back. So why don't you just return them and save the scene."

He didn't respond, just stalked from the room in three long strides.

She chased him into the hall. "Where do you think you're going?"

"I'm having a look around. And I don't want you sneaking off before I get back."

"Fine." Let him enjoy his sense of being in charge. She didn't need her keys until she was ready to go. She strode back to her room, and a moment later his voice drifted up to her.

"You *are* planning to lift prints from the area where the note was found, right?"

She tensed. Now he was giving Tommy a hard time. He needed to just butt out, go on home and stay out of her business.

But it wasn't Tommy who responded.

"Look, sonny. How about I don't go up to Memphis and tell you how to do your job, and you don't come down here and tell me how to do mine."

Chris didn't respond, but the door slammed so hard it jarred the pictures on the front bedroom wall, announcing exactly what he thought of Branch's haughty comeback. The whole exchange would have given her some satisfaction if she didn't dislike Branch so much.

She returned to the task at hand, first phoning the office to get her day's work covered and let them know she wouldn't be back. She would mail any transcripts that hadn't been done yet and leave her tapes and steno notes for the others. She hated to do it—she loved her job. This creep had taken too much from her. At first it was her peace of mind.

Now it was her home, her livelihood and her whole way of life.

She grabbed another box and emptied the last dresser drawer. Footsteps sounded on the stairs, but she didn't slow her pace. The closet was next. She swung open the doors and had just started to pull clothes from hangers when Chris's voice stopped her. It was low, tense, filled with dread.

"Missy, you'd better take a look at this. And bring a flashlight."

Her heart pounded in her chest, and she turned slowly to face him. She didn't want to know what he had found. She just wanted to escape, to run as far away as possible and forget about Harmony Grove and all its ghosts. But even as her mind screamed its objections, she lifted her gaze to meet his.

And the fear she saw there turned her blood to ice.

# FIFTEEN

She followed him out the back door and across the yard at a half run, then hesitated at the open door of the stable. It was worse than she remembered. The roof was sagging even deeper, ready to cave in with the next heavy rain. The wooden panels that made up its walls were rotted through in several places, and the metal rolling door rested at a cockeyed angle, well off its track.

She looked at Chris with raised brows. "You expect me to go inside?"

"I wouldn't try to take up residence there, but I think it'll hold up another few hours."

He stepped over the metal track, and she followed him into the dingy interior. Two bales of hay sat against the far wall, covered by a horse blanket. Wasn't there a third bale at one point?

"What am I supposed to be looking for?"

"Check the stalls."

She moved deeper into the shadows. The heavy wooden awning at the back of the first stall was dropped in an effort to keep out rain—an effort that was futile considering the state of the roof. Rusted-out panels had pulled apart, and narrow slashes of sunlight pierced the gaps. She clicked on the flashlight and swept its beam around the compartment. It held odd sizes of plywood and varying lengths of two-by-fours. The second stall was empty.

When she shined the light into the last stall, a wave of goose bumps cascaded over her skin. The roof was in better shape there—at least the back portion of it—and someone had set up housekeeping. A low platform stood in the left rear corner, covered in blankets with a pillow at one end, likely her third bale of hay. Short lengths of two-by-fours topped by a small piece of plywood formed a makeshift table that occupied the opposite corner. Several objects littered its top.

"Dennis." The name was a hushed whisper.

Chris looked at her sharply. "Who's Dennis?"

"Mrs. Johnson's grandson. He asked if he could stay in the stable. I told him no, but I guess he decided to move in anyway."

"Do you think he has anything to do with what's been going on?"

"No, I don't. I mean, he's a major mooch and has a boulder-sized chip on his shoulder, but he doesn't seem crazy." She stepped into the space and studied the items scattered about the table—a pair of rubber gloves, a flashlight, a box of matches, a single-burner propane camp stove, a variety of pencils, a sketch pad lying haphazardly across a book…and an

MP3 player identical to the one she had misplaced. Her eyes widened, and her heart pounded an erratic rhythm in her chest. Was this *her* MP3 player, taken from inside the house?

She touched the corner of the sketch pad, careful not to disturb any fingerprints that may have been left, and tried to flip back the front cover with a single finger. The pad slid over and exposed the book underneath—the same book that had disappeared from her bedside stand. Her heart beat harder. It was a bestseller, with thousands of copies in circulation. But both the MP3 player *and* the book? It was too far-fetched to be mere coincidence.

She spun around and threw back the blanket covering the platform. The familiarity of the pillowcase barely registered before something else caught her eye: a piece of lavender silk. Her missing nightgown. She gasped and stumbled backward. Now there was no doubt. She wasn't crazy. Someone had come into the house.

And Dennis had access to his grandmother's key.

With that new realization, a sickening lump formed in her gut. Dennis had used the key to let himself in. He had watched her while she slept, left notes and taken her things. Mrs. Johnson would be crushed.

She turned to tell Chris what she found, but the words stuck in her throat. He was bent over the sketch pad, now open, and glanced up at her. Deep furrows marked the space between his brows, and fear filled that dark gaze. Dread trickled over her, a thick black ooze that held her immobile. What could possibly be in the notebook to put that look on his face?

"Chris?"

He flipped back to the first page, and she prodded herself forward to look at what was there. Her own face stared back at her, and she had a sudden sense of having stepped into an alternate reality. The sketch was done in charcoal, perfect in every detail, each contour of her face, every wave of her hair. If Dennis hoped to be a successful artist someday, his dreams were well within reach.

She glanced up at Chris. "Dennis is an artist. And until two days before you moved in, he lived in the garage apartment. His grandmother is the only person who has a key besides the Tylers and me. So everything points to him." Somehow, that was much less terrifying than thinking Eugene had found her. But she couldn't let down her guard. Dennis was crazy—the notes proved that—and possibly dangerous. A new thought added to the dread already swirling inside her. "He could walk in on us, and we'd be trapped."

He put an arm across her shoulders and pulled her close. Warmth radiated from him, chasing away some of the chill that had seeped into her bones the moment she entered the stall.

"It's okay," he promised, his voice soothing. "Before coming to get you, I checked to make sure no one was hiding. I found tire tracks on the other side of your back fence. Someone's been coming off the main road outside of town and cutting through the field behind your place. That's why no one's seen anything. But we'll hear him if he comes back."

Chris was right. With Dennis's souped-up muscle car, stealth would be impossible. She angled the beam of the flashlight on the pad and slowly turned the pages. Each bore a sketch of her, depicted from various angles, all from the shoulders up. Then there was one of her weeding her garden and another of her walking up the front sidewalk.

As she studied the next series of pictures, bile rose in her throat. She was lying in bed, sound asleep—on her right side, on her left, on her back, comforter pulled to her chin, then thrown down around her waist. An image settled in her mind—Dennis standing next to her bed, eyes raking over her while she slept. She brushed a palm down each arm, longing to wash away the remnants of his lewd gaze, all the while knowing twenty hot showers wouldn't change the way she felt.

"If I ever get my hands on this creep..." Chris pulled her closer still, holding her as if he would never let go.

She turned another page. This sketch was different from the others. Instead of being alone, she was joined by a man. As before, every detail was perfect. But that was where reality ended.

The man wore a tunic covered in fancy embroidery and beadwork and fitted trousers that disappeared into knee-high boots. A leather mask covered the upper half of his face, and mildly unkempt locks fell past his shoulders, long but amazingly masculine.

Her clothing was just as out of place. A simple gown flowed around her ankles, molded tightly over her hips by an embroidered and beaded belt that complemented his tunic. The rib-crushing, low-cut bodice was also elaborately decorated, its primary purpose to force a good portion of her bosom above the gathered edge of the gown's plunging neckline. They stood holding hands, their backdrop a field of wildflowers and a distant castle.

The other sketches were equally bizarre. She was depicted with the same mystery man, sharing a drink from what looked like a gold chalice, eating at a long, wooden table heavily laden with food, dancing under a starlit sky. The settings were rich, the costumes elaborate—a lord and his lady.

Then the tone changed from opulent and festive to simple and serious. They were both barefoot, their clothing unadorned. Her simple, thin gown billowed about her legs, and a wreath of flowers encircled her head. A common thread ran through these final pages—adoration, sincerity and reverence, all captured in charcoal. Each sketch depicted a different part of the same somber ceremony, ending with the two of them in waist-deep water, hands joined.

Melissa closed the back cover and hauled in a shaky breath. Except for the first few pages, the entire book was a bizarre fantasy right out of the imagination of a madman.

And she had won the leading role.

"Do you recognize the man in the sketches?"

Melissa sighed. "With just a mouth and chin to go on, I'm afraid I don't. It could be anybody."

"What about the hair? Do you know any men with hair like that?"

She gave a dry laugh. "Yeah, Mel Gibson in *Braveheart*. But I don't think Dennis is going for realism here. The long hair is just part of the fantasy, along with the creative costumes."

Chris dropped his arm from her shoulders. "Tommy and Branch just left, but we'll call them back. The sooner they pick up this Dennis character, the better I'll feel."

She nodded and followed him toward the house, an odd sense of relief filling her chest. She was still in danger. Her stalker hadn't been caught, and not only was he watching her and leaving notes, but he was bold enough to come inside while she slept, which made him even more dangerous. But she finally knew she wasn't crazy. And soon the entire Harmony Grove Police Department would, too.

"You know," she began once they were inside, "the night of the storm when I thought I saw someone standing in my doorway, I bet it was Dennis. This also explains why I kept finding Smudge under the bed. Animals sense things, and I think Dennis really freaked him out."

"Smart cat."

"And," she added, "the gloves explain why there were never any prints."

"Hopefully he wasn't so careful in the stable."

Chris was right. Without prints, there wouldn't be enough evidence to hold him.

A few minutes later, Tommy stood on her porch. He was alone. Branch had evidently decided to stay at the station. "Did you find something?"

"We did," she answered. "And we're pretty sure we know who's behind all this." She took a deep breath, then hesitated. What if she was wrong? What if it wasn't Dennis?

But it had to be.

She led him down the walk and around the end of the house. All the proof she needed was in the stable. The mystery was solved. Within days it would be over. The cops would have their man. And she had no doubt it was the right one. He had access to the key. He wanted to move in. He was an artist. There was no one else it could be.

So why the nagging suspicion that she was making a terrible, terrible mistake?

Chris sat up slowly and twisted side to side, trying to work the stiffness out of his back, while Smudge watched from an adjacent upholstered chair. The antique damask sofa looked quaint and rich. But it made a lousy bed. The only reason he had chosen it was its proximity to the front door.

He had gotten Missy to safety, left her his Blazer,

then returned in her car after dark. And all night long, he waited, gun lying on the coffee table next to him and ears tuned for the slightest sound, even while he dozed. He was hoping Dennis would come back and use the front door, as he had the previous night. Now he understood the amazing disappearing act—Dennis had used his grandmother's key to slip into the house, then locked the door behind him.

And all the while, Missy had slept inside, so sure, since the doors and windows were locked, that she was safe. And he'd trudged back to the garage apartment and gone to bed, unknowingly leaving her in the worst possible danger. He hadn't stopped kicking himself since.

With a sigh, he pushed himself to his feet, and the cat jumped down to make several passes against his shins. "Well, good morning, Smudge. I hope you slept better than I did."

Smudge meowed a response, then pranced toward the kitchen with several glances back. The cat clearly expected him to follow.

"I know, I know, it's breakfast time."

Missy had made him promise to take good care of her cat. And he didn't mind a bit. Letting her stay in the house was out of the question, and he didn't want her running away. So he had convinced her to stay with BethAnn and Kevin. The prior afternoon, they moved her computer and a few pieces of clothing and personal items. If Dennis wasn't picked up soon, they would have to go back for more.

As soon as he had Smudge fed and watered, he placed a call to Melissa. Judging from the lively lilt to her voice, she had been up for a while.

"Any sign of Dennis?" she asked.

"I'm afraid not. I was so ready for him to use his key and come on in. But he never showed. Maybe he saw me drive up and knew it was me instead of you, even though it was your car sitting in the driveway."

A sigh came through the phone, heavy with disappointment, and he couldn't help but feel he had let her down.

"I'm going to get this guy, Missy. Just give me time."

"Don't worry. I won't go anywhere. At least for the time being." She drew in a deep breath. "How's Smudge?"

"In the kitchen, smacking happily."

"Good." There was a smile in her tone. "Thanks for taking care of him for me."

"I'm happy to do it. So what's on your agenda for today?"

"Transcription."

"You're staying home?"

"Yep, chained to the computer all day long."

Uneasiness stirred in his chest. "Is someone going to be with you?"

"No. BethAnn's leaving for her store in a few minutes, and Kevin's already gone."

The uneasiness intensified. "You shouldn't stay home alone. I'd stay with you myself, but Sam has classes and Derrick is still on his honeymoon. Karen's too new to leave her alone."

"Chris, I don't need a babysitter. As soon as BethAnn leaves, I'll lock myself in. Dennis doesn't have access to BethAnn's key."

He nodded slowly. BethAnn's house was safer than the Tyler place. But it was still Harmony Grove. And she was still alone. "How about if you hang out at my place today instead?"

"I can't. I'm not going to waste a whole day of transcription time. After quitting with no notice yesterday, I'm just thankful I still have a job. Fortunately, I have an understanding boss."

"Well, if they haven't picked up Dennis by tonight, I'd like to move you to my dad's place. Dennis won't look for you in Lakeland."

A long span passed in silence. Finally she sighed. "All right. If it'll make you feel better, I'll do it. And I'll keep my phone by the computer. Anytime you're worried about me, you can call me."

"If I called you every time I worried about you, it wouldn't be worth hanging up."

"You've got a point there." The smile was back. "Maybe that isn't such a good plan, since we both hope to get something accomplished today."

# SIXTEEN

Melissa popped a bite of scrambled egg into her mouth and turned on her computer. Days like this were welcome—several hours of uninterrupted time to get caught up on transcription. Well, uninterrupted except for frequent calls from Chris. But that was all right. Finally, for the first time in weeks, there was hope—a sliver of light at the end of a long, dark tunnel.

She pushed aside her now empty plate, ready to tackle the day's tasks. Within moments, the whine of a distant siren hauled her mind away from the words on the screen. It screamed closer, then abruptly ceased, leaving a silence as jarring as the piercing wail had been. Moments later, a second emergency vehicle approached.

As she leaned toward the monitor, comparing the transcribed sentences on the left with the steno shorthand on the right, apprehension nibbled at the edges of her mind. She scrolled through another page, cleaning up an occasional sloppy stroke and adding missed punctuation. Her anxiety intensified. The eggs and biscuits that had tasted so good lay heavy in her gut, a doughy lump.

A third wail pierced the early-morning stillness, and she glanced at her watch. The sirens probably had nothing to do with Chris, but she couldn't shake the uneasiness. Twenty minutes earlier, he had stopped to leave her car and pick up his Blazer. He should be almost to work by now.

She pushed herself away from the computer and picked up the phone. Chris would tease her, but so be it. He had done plenty of worrying himself in recent weeks.

Four rings later, his phone went to voice mail. Her stomach tightened into a solid knot. Why wasn't he answering? She walked out of BethAnn's office and stared at the front door, pulling her lower lip between her teeth. She had promised Chris she wouldn't leave the house. But she had to do something.

She hesitated only a moment longer, then grabbed her purse and dashed out the door. The activity helped hold the anxiety at bay. But the reprieve didn't last long. When she turned to head out of town, the road ahead disappeared under a halo of flashing red and blue. Apprehension descended on her again, this time with a vengeance. She jammed the accelerator to the floor.

*Dear God, please don't let it be Chris.*

A block from the intersection, a sheriff's vehicle sat diagonally in the road. The premonition grew stronger as she braked to a stop. Beyond the cruiser, a dump truck carrying a full load of sand sat at an odd angle. Its buckled hood and mangled front grille glinted in the early-morning sunlight. An ambulance and fire truck waited nearby, lights strobing their disturbing rhythm. Where was the other vehicle?

The deputy stopped her the moment she stepped from the car. "Ma'am, you need to turn around."

"What did the truck hit?" She had to know.

"Ma'am, you need to leave." The firmness in his tone carried a warning.

She glanced around, looking for Alan or Tommy. At this point, even Chief Branch would do. But the only other law enforcement vehicle at the scene was another sheriff car. Of course, this was outside city limits. Harmony Grove police wouldn't have been called.

She turned her attention back to the deputy. "Please. My friend just came this way."

He looked her over, and the stern lines of his face seemed to soften. "The other vehicle was a black Blazer."

Her uneasiness was replaced by full-blown panic. She raced around the deputy and his parked car, covering the last block at a run. When she rounded the front of the ambulance, her knees buckled. The driver's side had taken the full impact. The front quarter panel and both doors were a mangled mass of metal. The windshield was shattered, and the glass that had made up the side windows was completely gone. Two bumper stickers proclaimed, Fun Begins at Jamison Marine, and Gold's Gym, personalizing the vehicle as effectively as a vanity plate.

*Dear God, please let him be all right.*

She rushed forward, heart pounding in her chest, then stopped dead as all the strength drained from her limbs. Chris was slumped against the seat belt, unconscious. Several rivulets of blood had traced sticky paths down his face and onto his shirt, and a large plastic brace encircled his neck. One paramedic was on his knees in the front passenger seat, working to extricate him, while a second waited at the open passenger door.

"Chris," she whispered, and reached out to touch his cheek.

The paramedic inside the truck stopped her. "Stand back, ma'am."

She withdrew her hand and pressed it to her mouth. As they pulled him across the seat and lowered him onto a spine board, tears welled up, and regret pressed down on her. She had been so concerned with protecting her heart she had never told him how she felt. *God, please give us another chance.*

"Is he going to be okay?"

Two paramedics hoisted the board while a third opened the ambulance doors. "We're taking him to Lakeland Regional. They'll be able to answer your questions there."

As she watched them drive away, lights flashing and sirens wailing, hot tears pushed their way forward and pooled on her lashes. One escaped to trace a wet path down her cheek, and she swiped it away. This wasn't the time to break down. Since she wouldn't be allowed to see him for a while, maybe she could get some answers.

A sheriff's deputy and another gentleman stood nearby, the deputy making notes on his pad while the other man talked. When they seemed to be finished, she approached them.

"My friend was driving the Blazer. Can you tell me what happened?"

The man's face crumpled, and distress crept into his warm brown eyes. The embroidered patch over his left shirt pocket matched the name on the truck. "I'm so sorry. I tried to stop, but there wasn't time."

"What happened? Did he pull out in front of you?"

"No, he ran right through the stop sign, never slowed down." The truck driver shook his head, anguish etched into the lines of his face. "All of a sudden he was there in front of me. A fraction of a second later, I hit him." He shifted his weight from one foot to the other as he talked, gesturing awkwardly. "I hardly even had time to go for the brake."

"He drove *through* the stop sign?"

"He did. Never even slowed down."

That didn't make sense. Chris would have turned left to go to work. Had he lied about where he was going? She thanked the deputy and truck driver and hiked back to her car. The rest of her questions would have to be answered by Chris.

Before the day's end, she would get to the bottom of this.


Chris floated on the edge of consciousness, thoughts he couldn't quite grasp drifting through his mind. A series of beeps came from somewhere in the distance. Voices, too. Female. One he didn't recognize. The other was familiar. It sounded like Missy. Where was he? He should probably open his eyes, but they were so heavy. All he wanted to do was sleep.

His head hurt, though. So did his back. In fact, he felt stiff and achy all over. He forced his eyes open just as a woman hung a bag on a metal rack. It had clear fluid inside and a tube sticking out of the bottom. Like an IV bag. His gaze drifted back to the woman…to her eyes. She had kind eyes. Eyes that suddenly met his and widened.

"Well, look who decided to join us."

Join who? Where was he? He studied the woman with the kind eyes, looking for answers. She was wearing a nurse's uniform. Was she there for him?

Before he could ponder it further, she walked away and someone else stepped into his line of vision. Missy. He tried to look more fully in her direction, but couldn't turn his head. What was stopping him? He reached to touch his neck, and his hand met hard plastic. Some kind of brace.

"How do you feel?"

He didn't respond. Answering the simplest questions required too much concentration. "What happened?"

"You had an accident. But you're going to be okay."

An accident? Why couldn't he remember?

"It was pretty bad," Missy continued. "You drove out in front of a truck."

An image flashed into his mind. Nothing before, nothing after. Just a single, disjointed memory—a very large grille right outside his driver's side window. "I think... I think I remember."

"Where were you going?"

"I don't know." He searched the pathways of his mind for the information she wanted. It was stored in there somewhere. He just had to find it. He would have left home—no, wait. He didn't leave from home. He left from Missy's, picked up his Blazer at Beth-Ann's. And he was going to work. "I was headed to the store."

Missy's brows creased. "But you went straight. You didn't go left toward Lakeland."

"I don't remember." He tried to shift his position and grimaced.

She flashed him a sympathetic smile. "They've got you strapped to a spine board."

"I think I've got a flat spot on the back of my head, and my wallet is permanently imprinted on my rear."

"They've got to look at your X-rays and CAT scan before they let you off of it."

"I've already had X-rays *and* a CAT scan?"

"You slept through them."

The scrape of metal against metal cut their conversation short as the curtain was pulled back in its curved track. The same nurse appeared. "I have someone who needs to see you."

She stepped aside, and a moment later, a uniformed deputy stood next to him. He held a clipboard in one hand and a pen in the other.

"Do you feel up to answering a few questions?"

"I've had better days, but I think I can handle it."

"I'll try to make it as painless as possible." The smile he flashed him was almost boyish. Actually, everything about him was boyish. Slightly chunky, with a roundish face, he looked like someone who should be delivering pizzas rather than traffic tickets. Except for the uniform.

He looked down at his clipboard. "I've already got your registration information, but I need to see your driver's license."

"I'm lying on it."

"On second thought, we'll save that for last. Why don't you tell me what happened?"

"It's kind of foggy. I'm not sure how much I can remember. I left where I was staying and was going to work." Except Missy said he wasn't headed toward Lakeland.

"And?" the deputy prompted.

Why did he go straight? Where was he going? "The brakes." Suddenly he remembered. "I was coming up to the stop sign, and when I hit my brakes, they weren't working. I went for the emergency brake, but by then I was already in the path of the truck."

"I see." The deputy wrote feverishly in his pad. "When did you last have your brakes worked on?"

"About a month ago. I had the rotors turned and new pads put on all four wheels."

"Well, I'm going to give you the benefit of the doubt and cite you for faulty equipment instead of running the stop sign."

Suddenly Melissa gasped. "Dennis!"

Chris looked at her sharply.

"The last note said something about spilling the other man's blood."

She was right. There was no way to know for sure without checking his truck. But he would bet his last dollar the brake lines had been cut. Except there was one problem. "My Blazer was parked at BethAnn and Kevin's all night."

"Maybe he found me at BethAnn's and saw your truck there. Or maybe he cut them at Mrs. Johnson's, you know, just enough of a break for the fluid to leak out slowly, and it wasn't until that last stop that the brakes actually failed."

He nodded slowly, then filled the deputy in on all that had happened.

"Has a report been made on this?"

"Several of them. In fact, the Harmony Grove Police Department has all these notes in evidence."

The deputy made several notations on his paperwork and put his pen back into his shirt pocket. "I'm going to hold on to this until we do some further investigating. I'll be in touch."

As soon as the deputy left, a doctor entered the room. At least, that's who he assumed she was, with her white coat, clipboard and stethoscope around her neck. "Well, Mr. Jamison," she began, "your X-rays look pretty good. You're going to be quite sore for a few days, but there aren't any fractures or dislocations. I *am* concerned about the head injury though, so I'm going to keep you overnight for observation." She lowered the clipboard she had consulted and stepped closer to the bed. "We'll be moving you to a room shortly. Meanwhile, are you ready to part with the neck brace and this comfortable board?"

"You have no idea."

Once the board was gone and the doctor left the room, he reached for Missy's hand. "I'm glad they got hold of you. It was nice to wake up and see your face."

"Wellll…" She stretched out the word and hoisted both shoulders. The gesture was accompanied by a sheepish smile. "They didn't exactly call me. I heard sirens after you left and had a really uneasy feeling. When you didn't answer your phone, I had to make sure you were okay."

He shook his head in disapproval. "You ladies and your women's intuition. I should scold you for reneging on your promise. But under the circumstances, I guess it was understandable. So how bad was it?"

"It was bad. The driver's side of your truck was

so mangled, they had to pull you out the passenger's side. That's what they were doing when I got there. You were unconscious and covered in blood." She shuddered at the memory. "I can't believe you weren't hurt worse."

"I know. God was really watching out for me."

Her jaw went slack. "You're crediting God with taking care of you?"

"Don't look so shocked. God isn't just some distant, way-out-there God, you know. He's close and personal and cares about every aspect of our lives." His smile was teasing, but he meant every word.

She returned his grin. "That sounds vaguely familiar, like I've heard it before."

"A wise lady once told me that, and I took it to heart."

"She must have been *very* wise."

"*Very* wise," he repeated. "And very beautiful."

Her eyes filled with emotion, and he longed to pull her closer, to wrap her in his arms and never let her go. But he tamped down the thought. He had said he would wait until she was ready, and whatever it took, he was going to keep that promise.

"So what are your plans for the rest of the day?"

She dropped his hand and looked at her watch. "I'm going to leave here and get back on my transcription."

His stomach clenched, and dread settled in his chest. "You can't go back there alone. If Dennis knows where you've gone, you'll be in as much danger there as at the Tyler place."

She thought for several moments. "I'll find out what time Kevin will be home. He always starts early in the morning so he can be through before the worst heat of the day." She scrolled through her contacts and put the phone to her ear. A short time later, she snapped it closed and dropped it back into her purse. "He'll be home within the hour."

He shook his head. "I still don't like it. As soon as I get out of here, I'm moving you to my place."

"And what about you? You can't go back to Harmony Grove."

Determination coursed through his veins. "I'm going to catch this guy, Missy."

"I don't want you to try to catch him. Let Alan and Tommy do it. You're in more danger than I am."

"How do you figure that?"

"He hasn't even hinted at hurting me."

He stifled a snort. "No, he just wants to kidnap you."

"But he tried to kill you."

He studied her for several moments, a ready argument on the tip of his tongue. But the concern in that pleading gaze softened his retort. If the tables were turned, he would have a fit about her going back. "I'll have to think about it."

She didn't have a chance to object to his noncommittal answer. A male nurse entered the room and pulled the curtain fully open. "How about we move you to a real room with a real bed?"

"Sounds good." He turned back to Missy. "Are you coming up?"

"By the time I find my way to my car and make it back to Harmony Grove, Kevin will be home. So I'm going to get back to work and let you get some rest."

"I've had plenty of sleep," he argued. "I was out for a good hour or two." He once again snagged her hand.

"I'll be back this evening."

"I don't know." He affected a grave tone. "You think I'll make it that long without you?"

A teasing smile touched her mouth. "Don't worry—you won't be alone. I'm sure someone will be in every hour to poke you or take your blood pressure."

"Thanks for the encouragement, but that wasn't the kind of attention I was hoping for."

She waved with her free hand, and he released her.

It was going to be a long afternoon.

# SEVENTEEN

Melissa pushed Chris down the hall in a hospital wheelchair, heels echoing against the vinyl tile.

"I don't know why I have to leave in this thing." He shifted in the chair and heaved a frustrated sigh. A day and a half in the hospital obviously hadn't sat well with him. She had never seen him so antsy.

"Because letting you walk out of here is a liability. If you get dizzy and crack your head open, they don't want to be sued."

"Well, it makes me feel like an invalid."

"Poor baby. A little humility is good for you."

He craned his neck to look up at her. "Hey, I'm a humble enough guy."

"Well, you were almost a *dead* guy." She stopped in front of a bank of elevators and punched the down button. "But I've got some good news. On my way up here, I talked to Tommy, and they've found Dennis. He's being taken in for questioning. So I can go back home, and you can, too."

"I think we should go ahead with our plans until we know for sure everything is resolved."

She wheeled him through the open elevator doors. Maybe he was right. Dennis had been picked up, and Tommy had lifted prints from the stable and sent them off to the Florida Department of Law Enforcement. But the results hadn't come back yet.

"All right," she agreed. "We've got to pick up Smudge on the way home." As soon as she'd gotten back to Harmony Grove the prior day, she and Kevin had taken him to Harmony Grove Pet Resort. "We also need to get you a rental car. Then we'll get my stuff packed." Making the move now seemed like an exercise in futility, but if it made Chris feel better, she would go along with it. At least he had agreed to stay away from Harmony Grove once he got her moved. Instead, he would be living with neighbors two doors down from the Lakeland house.

By the time they pulled into her driveway, the sun sat low in the sky. The hospital didn't release Chris until midafternoon, and the rental car had just come back in and wasn't quite ready. Even the pet resort was swamped; a full fifteen minutes passed before anyone was free to go to the back and retrieve Smudge. Then they had to go to BethAnn's and repack everything they had unpacked two nights ago. Now that Smudge was being displaced, too, she needed to pick up his things, besides getting a few more items for herself.

Chris frowned at her, creases of tension lining his face. "Let's make this quick. I really wanted to be away from here before now."

She brought Smudge inside, then put Chris to work cleaning the litter box and gathering cat food while she tackled her clothes and personal belongings. When they stepped out the door with the last of the bags, the sun had long ago dipped beneath the horizon. She slid into the driver's seat with Smudge in her arms and watched Chris place a bag of cans on the front floorboard. "What about the bag of dry cat food?"

"I got the cans together and forgot all about the dry. Lock the doors. I'll be right back."

Smudge settled onto her lap and started to purr. Once they left, he would have to lie in the passenger's seat. But he wouldn't be a problem; he wasn't afraid of car rides. Actually, there wasn't much Smudge *was* afraid of. Except Dennis.

The ringing of her cell phone interrupted her thoughts.

"Melissa, are you with Chris?" The voice belonged to Tommy Willis.

"Sort of. He's inside. Why?"

"You guys need to leave. We got a match on the prints, and they don't belong to Dennis."

"They don't? But who…"

Her voice trailed off as the metallic clicks of the locks drew her attention. But not for long because Smudge chose that moment to go berserk. He scrambled up the front of her and lunged for the window, making contact with a thud. Before she had a chance to react, he shot across the car and out the now open passenger door, disappearing in a flurry of fur and claws. She gasped and dropped the phone into her lap, grasping, too late, for the cat.

Then her gaze locked on one tanned, muscled arm, and she stopped breathing altogether. An elaborately inked bald eagle stared back, a wicked glint in its beady blue-black eyes. A wave of horror crashed down on her. She knew that tattoo. What the artist had intended as a symbol of strength, pride and power had for her become the embodiment of terror.

Eugene dropped a set of keys into the console and slid the rest of the way into the car, one hand braced against the inside edge of the seat. Muscles rippled and bulged beneath the inked design, bringing the malevolent creature to life. Panic spiraled through her, and she sat frozen—mute, paralyzed, her mind locked. When his other arm came around, her blood froze in her veins. That hand held a pistol.

"Hang up the phone." The hushed whisper penetrated the fog, and her gaze dropped to her lap. Tommy was saying something, probably telling her that the prints belonged to one Eugene Holmes and detailing the rap sheet he had. She couldn't make out the words. They wouldn't have registered anyway, even if she held the phone to her ear. Her brain had shut down the instant her gaze locked on to that tattoo. She slowly closed the phone.

Eugene touched the gun lightly to her shoulder and traced a line down her bare arm, leaving a tingling path, fire and ice at the same time. "My sweet

Melissa. At last, our time is here. I have fought valiantly and won against all odds. And now I'm claiming my prize."

She lifted her gaze, steeling herself for the rage simmering beneath that cool exterior. It wasn't there. Instead, his eyes held a dull vacancy, as if the soul behind them was missing. He was completely insane.

She started to reach for her door handle, but froze as the pistol retraced its path up her arm. It came to rest against her right temple, and she dropped her hand to her side. "How did you find me?"

A glimmer of life flickered in his pale gray eyes. "My brother helped me. But you didn't make it easy."

His brother? She didn't know he had a brother.

"You were meant to be with me." His voice carried almost no inflection. "It's your destiny. If I don't help you fulfill it, I'm not deserving of you." He glanced toward the house, and as he spoke, the pistol slowly followed his gaze. "I know now what is required of me. I must spill the other man's blood. And when I do, remember, I'm doing it all for you. That is the depth of my love for you."

The panic that careened through her system lodged in her mind, scattering her thoughts in a thousand different directions. She was trapped in a nightmare and couldn't wake up. Eugene was going to kill Chris. Somehow, she had to stop him.

"Get ready." The lifeless tone continued. "As soon as it's done, we leave. Yesterday I failed. I searched half the night for his car, and when I heard sirens the next morning, I was sure my plan had worked. Tonight I won't fail."

She cast a frantic glance at the house. Lights were still on inside. But at any moment, it would fall into darkness, and Chris would step out the door.

*Lord, please help me do this right.*

She summoned her best powers of persuasion and jammed the key into the ignition. "We need to leave now. If you fire the gun, someone will try to stop us."

The house went dark. Panic surged anew. She turned the key, and music from the CD player flooded the interior. *Lord, help me,* she pleaded again, and shoved the transmission into Reverse. Hard. Tires spun against gravel. The car lurched to a stop. *Come on, let's go, let's go.* She restarted the engine and backed toward the stable, pulse pounding in her ears. The front door swung open. She shoved the transmission into first and flew down the gravel drive, disappearing between the trees before Chris stepped onto the porch.

*Thank You, Lord.* The first hurdle was cleared—Chris was safe. Now she only had herself to worry about.

Her phone began to ring in her lap, and she glanced down at the glowing screen. Tommy probably just realized she was gone and was dialing back. She looked at Eugene for direction, but he simply turned away to lower the window. The next instant, he snatched the phone off her lap and tossed it from the car, effectively cutting her off from the rest of the world. Hopelessness washed over her. Even if she could escape, she couldn't call for help.

She eased to a stop at an intersection outside of town, the scene of Chris's accident the prior day. An old Chevy was parked on the other side of the road. She didn't need to see the Georgia plate to know it was Eugene's.

"Go straight." He gave the command without the slightest hesitation. Evidently he had a plan.

She didn't. Hers had ended the moment she left her driveway.

She had been so wrong. It had been easy to blame Dennis. He was right next door, he had access to a key and he was an artist. Blaming him kept her from facing the alternative, that it was Eugene leaving the notes, coming into her house, watching her as she slept.

But how... She shot a glance his direction. "How have you been getting in?"

"Your spare key."

"Did Dennis—" No, that was impossible. Eugene didn't know Dennis. But there wasn't any other explanation. The Tylers had given her two keys. One stayed on her key ring, and the other was on her closet shelf, along with her spare car key. She would have known if someone had broken in and stolen the keys. Yet somehow Eugene had both.

An image flashed across her mind, a gaping hole, surrounded by jagged shards of glass. "You broke my family room window, didn't you? It wasn't a branch."

He turned toward her. The darkness was too deep to see his face, but when he spoke, she would swear there was a smile hidden in the dull tone. "I used a rock, then dragged a branch under the window. I've gotten quite clever, you know."

Still holding the gun in his right hand, he reached around with his left to move her hair back over her shoulder. Midway through an automatic recoil, she froze, then forced herself to sit still while his fingers kneaded the stiff muscles of her neck.

"You're tense," he observed. "Why are you tense?" He continued after the briefest pause, still massaging her neck. "You know, there's nothing to be afraid of. I love you and only want what's best for you."

Maybe she could appeal to that love, however warped it was. "If you really love me, let me go home."

"No!"

She flinched at the anger in his tone, desperately wishing she could take back the words she had just spoken. When he continued, some of the sharpness was gone, but what he said put a solid knot of fear in her stomach. "You can never go home. You belong to me now. Tonight will seal it. I've won you, and no one is going to come between us ever again."

He fell silent, and she shifted uncomfortably in the seat. Her legs, stomach, chest—the whole front of her was on fire, throbbing from several deep scratches left by Smudge during his frantic escape from the car.

Hopefully he didn't go far. Maybe Chris had already recaptured him and put him safely inside.

She drew in a deep breath and let it out slowly. The soothing strains of her praise and worship CD filled the car, and she tried to draw strength from its message. How had she gotten it so wrong? He had fooled her. And finding the sketch pad had only thrown her further off track. Dennis was the artist. Not Eugene. In all the weeks of knowing Eugene, there was nothing to indicate he knew how to draw.

Her eyes widened as another image flashed into her mind. Eugene and his ever-present notebook. She never saw him without it. Now she knew what was inside. He was an artist. The final piece of the puzzle fell into place. The only thing she didn't know was where he was taking her…and what he planned to do with her once they got there. He probably wouldn't tell her, but she would ask.

"Where are we going?"

His answer was an icy northern wind, penetrating so deep it chilled her soul.

"Paradise. We're going to paradise."

Chris paced the family room, trying to do more praying than worrying, but he wasn't successful. When he stepped from the house twenty minutes earlier, he felt as if he had just been beamed into the twilight zone. He had only been inside for a minute or two. But when he opened the door, Smudge flew past him into the house, a white streak, and Missy was gone.

For several moments, he stood on the porch in stunned disbelief. Then he kicked his befuddled brain into gear and dialed nine-one-one. He got Tommy, who promised to issue an APB and head right out. Then he set out to find BethAnn's number, no easy task since he didn't know Kevin's last name. The number would be in Missy's phone, but she had it with her. Fortunately, it was also in an address book he found in a kitchen drawer. He should have known she would have numbers stored somewhere besides her phone. Missy always had a backup plan.

He strode to the living room and flipped the switch. Soft light chased the shadows from the room. Missy's blazer lay over the end of the couch, evidently deposited there after work and forgotten. He picked it up and buried his face in the soft fabric, breathing in the spicy-sweet aroma of her perfume.

What happened to her? She wouldn't have left willingly. Someone forced his way into the car and gave her no other choice. And it wasn't Dennis. He was in custody. The only other possibility sent a cold blade of fear slicing through him. He had worked too many cases like this. And they rarely ended well. How could he have let it happen? *Please, God,* he pleaded. She couldn't end up just being another statistic.

He sank to his knees in front of the couch, her jacket clutched tightly in his fists. They had just found each other again. A bright, happy future was within their grasp. Adrianne robbed them of five years. Was Eugene going to rob them of the rest of their lives? *Dear God, please bring her back to me.*

White light flashed brightly through the living room window, and he sprang to his feet. Two vehicles moved up the driveway. One belonged to BethAnn and Kevin. But the other…no, that wasn't Missy's Honda. He could hear it now, some kind of a souped-up sports car. He opened the door as Alan jumped from a '68 fastback Mustang, complete with chrome headers and jacked-up rear end.

"Is Melissa here?" Concern laced the young officer's tone.

BethAnn and Kevin piled out of Kevin's pickup truck, and the three of them hurried up the front walk.

"No, she's disappeared." Chris studied Alan for a moment. The officer knew something, something that upgraded the concern of a few moments ago to outright panic. "What's going on? Why are you here?"

"I'm not even on duty," Alan began. "I stopped by the station to talk to Tommy for a few minutes, and he had just gotten a match back on the prints. He called Melissa, and the call got dropped. When he called back, it went to voice mail. So I left him at the station and headed straight here."

"What did you find out about the prints?" Beth-Ann asked.

"It wasn't Dennis. The prints belong to a Eugene

Holloman, aka Eugene Hornsby, aka Eugene Hopkins and a couple other aliases."

The blood drained from BethAnn's face. "Eugene Holmes?"

"That's not one we know about, but that doesn't mean anything. This guy changes names like you and I change socks."

BethAnn began to wring her hands, which certainly didn't do anything to calm his own frayed nerves. "It's the same Eugene. I just know it."

Chris sucked in a slow breath and tamped down the panic that had mounted with every word out of Alan's mouth. The frantic former fiancé wanted to bury his head in the sand and not hear about the danger she was in. But the detective needed to learn every detail, anything that might help them solve the case. He leveled a steady gaze on Alan and spoke with a calmness he didn't feel. "Tell me what you know about this guy."

"He's got a long history of mental illness. He served in Iraq for four years, saw several of his buddies get blown away, started acting irrationally and eventually had to be discharged. He's been on military disability ever since, which has been about six years now. Roughly six months after coming stateside, he started following this girl. The story is just about identical to Melissa's, except he managed to get himself arrested a couple of times."

"And what happened to the girl?"

"She left. Packed up and moved to another state.

Anyway, about a year later he changed his name and did it again. When it happened a third time, the V.A. actually hospitalized him, treated him with psychotherapy and drugs. Once he seemed stable, they let him out, and he did all right for a few months. Then reports started coming in again from a lady who worked at a coffee shop, saying that one of her customers followed her home and wouldn't leave her alone. Even though he had given a fictitious name, the prints matched this Eugene Holloman. Before they could pick him up, the girl disappeared."

He leaned back against the closed front door, dread settling over him. "Did they ever find her?"

Alan's gaze traveled to his feet, and he stuffed both hands into his pockets.

"Come on, man," Chris prodded. "Tell me what you know."

"They found her a couple days later. Some fishermen snagged her. But Eugene had an alibi, and they didn't have enough evidence to convict him. His next victim also drowned. But it was ruled an accident. She lived on a lake, couldn't swim, and a neighbor had seen her standing alone on the dock earlier that evening. Once again, Eugene had an alibi. And that's the last anyone's heard from him. Until now."

Chris closed his eyes and clutched the doorjamb, one image forefront in his mind. The last sketch. Missy and her mystery man in waist-deep water.

"I'm going to the station to get my car," Alan announced. "I'm putting myself on duty."

He opened his eyes to see Alan already halfway down the walk, moving toward his Mustang at a half jog. "Start by checking the lakes."

A sense of hopelessness washed over him. Eugene had Missy. There was no doubt. And just as surely as he knew who had taken her, he knew what he intended to do.

He planned to drown her.

# EIGHTEEN

As Melissa neared Bartow, she racked her brain for a plan of escape. Calling nine-one-one was out of the question. Her phone lay discarded in some vacant field several miles back. And stopping at a red light in town and jumping from the car was a bad idea. Traffic was sparse, and she wasn't likely to outrun a bullet.

That left only one option. It was risky, but it could work. Once she left Bartow, she would accelerate, then veer off the road and slam into a tree. Eugene hadn't fastened his seat belt. Actually, she hadn't, either. But she, at least, had the steering wheel.

"Turn up here." Eugene's command jarred her from her thoughts. A traffic light lay ahead, with a convenience store at the corner.

"Here?" The optimism she had been grasping for finally kicked in. He was taking her into a neighborhood. Compared to the miles of cow pastures and phosphate mines that lay past town, it almost felt safe. *Thank You, Lord.*

Several turns later, he instructed her to stop near

the end of a loop. Upper-middle-class houses with well-manicured lawns lined the street. Two young boys played basketball in one of the driveways, their game illuminated by the glow of a floodlight mounted a few feet from the hoop.

"Do you think those boys will try to interfere with our plans?" He slowly rotated the gun.

Her heart fell with a sickening thud. *Dear Lord, no, not the children.*

He tucked the barrel of the pistol into the waist-band of his pants and pulled his shirt down over it. "We're going to get out of the car now, but I won't let them interfere."

The boys stopped their game to watch as she and Eugene stepped from the car and walked down the property line a few feet from where they stood. She held her breath, every muscle stiff with apprehension. Then the thud of the basketball against the concrete driveway and the *thunk* of hard rubber meeting the wooden backboard announced that the game had begun anew, and relief washed over her.

At the back of the two yards, a chain-link fence halted their progress. Eugene led her along its length until he found an opening large enough to push her through. After he scrambled over the top and dropped to the ground beside her, he held out his hand, palm up. She pretended not to notice.

"Melissa." It wasn't just her name; it was a repri-mand. She was a disobedient child being scolded by an unhappy parent.

She ignored the rebuke. "What?"

"You know what." The stern tone continued. "You're mine now. I've won you, and I want to hold your hand."

Meaty fingers intertwined with hers, sending the desire to jerk free screaming through her body. She tackled the urge, but the shudder that shook her shoulders ripped past that wall of control.

Eugene didn't seem to notice. He began to stroll, holding her hand firmly in his. A canal hugged the edge of the grassy field where they walked, disappearing into a lake at each end. In the distance, lights sporadically dotted the landscape, solitary beacons too far away to be comforting. When Eugene led her toward a concrete bridge that spanned the narrow stream, she recognized their surroundings. They had entered Mary Holland Park from the back side.

"I've scoured the area the past couple of weeks, looking for the perfect place for our union. This is where fate led me. I hope you're happy with it. My family has a long history here."

Her gaze darted to his face. Had he been to the park before? It was possible. He had spent a summer in Fort Meade, only fifteen minutes away. A small flicker of hope glimmered in the darkness. A memory from his childhood might help connect him with reality.

"Have you been here before?"

"I came here several times the summer I stayed with my cousin."

She searched for a common thread. "I didn't come here as a child, but I had a picnic here with my friend BethAnn last weekend."

He continued without acknowledging that she had spoken. "My uncle ruled this kingdom."

Her heart fell. Distorted childhood memories were worthless. Whatever connections he once had with reality had long been severed. He motioned skyward. "A full moon makes hearts turn to love."

*And brings out the loonies.* She lifted her gaze. He was right. The moon *was* full, a perfect sphere glowing bright white in a deep, rich sky. She had already noticed it. She just hadn't decided whether it was going to be her friend or her foe.

Still looking heavenward, he moved away from the lake and stepped onto a narrow road. What was once asphalt had deteriorated to a crumbly mixture of sand and gravel.

"I told you we would be together someday. This is our night, Melissa. And it's all taking place under the light of a full moon." Warmth filled his tone. Delight laced with anticipation. He smiled down at her, but there was nothing comforting in the gesture. His upper lip curled back, and his teeth gleamed white in the moonlight. "I'm taking you to my castle now."

"Castle?" She swallowed hard. He was caught in some fantasy world and had sucked her in with him. Whatever her role, she would play along. Eventually he would let down his guard, and she would be ready. "Where is your castle?"

"Right up there."

Straight ahead, the road disappeared under a metal gate, beyond which lay the soccer field. Inside the gate, he stopped.

"We need to catch our breath. We don't want to be winded for the procession."

"Procession?"

He looked at her with raised eyebrows. "Surely someone of your station has walked in dozens of processions."

She nodded slowly.

"Just follow my lead. You will walk with me up the path until we reach the top. There the people will witness our vows."

"What path?" she asked, and immediately regretted it.

Eugene grabbed her roughly by the shoulders and leaned over, his face inches from her own. Cold fury ran just beneath the surface, reflected in his steel-gray eyes. "The path leading up the hill to my castle. You see it, so don't try to tell me it's not there." His voice wasn't raised, but the tightness of his grip silenced her. So did the hardness in his tone, like steel striking flint. He released her shoulders and wrapped one meaty hand around her upper arm. "Now, are you going to cooperate?"

She didn't immediately respond. Her brain was stuck in neutral, and everything around her had an otherworldly feel. *If this is a nightmare, please wake me up.* How could he look at a flat, grassy field and see a hill with a path and a castle on top?

*BethAnn's fort.* A favorite play place bulldozed to make way for the soccer fields. For BethAnn, it held fond memories of playing make-believe with her childhood friends. Eugene had memories, too. But his spilled into the present, blurring the line between fantasy and reality.

His hand tightened painfully. Throbbing, needle-like sensations zinged down her arm and into her fingers, reminding her that she had been asked a question. She nodded vigorously.

"Good. It's time. Are you ready?"

Without waiting for an answer, he flexed his arm and lifted her hand to rest in the crook of his elbow. Then he took a step forward and stopped, another step and stopped. When they reached the center of the field, he turned to face her and grasped her hands. "Now we say our vows."

He stared down at her, and she averted her gaze. She could play the part, say the words and go through the motions. But her eyes would give it away—the fear she tried to hide, the revulsion, her thoughts of escape.

"Look at me," he commanded. "It's important that you look at me."

She dragged her eyes back to his. Maybe if she cleared her mind, thought only of… Chris. She would think of Chris. He was out there somewhere searching for her, frantic with worry. He would have alerted all the law enforcement agencies. And when he found her, he would draw her into his arms and hold her and kiss her, and she would never be afraid again.

Eugene squeezed her hands, and reality crashed back in. "I take thee, princess, into my care." His voice boomed out over the empty field, and she flinched. He was an actor onstage in a crowded theater, bellowing his lines to the farthest row. "I pledge you my love and protection, both in this life and in the one to come. I promise to be ever at your side and to destroy any forces that may try to come against us."

He fell silent and stared at her, waiting. What was she supposed to do?

"Go ahead," he whispered. "It's your turn."

"I—I'm a little nervous. I need you to help me."

"Just repeat what I say." She nodded, and he continued, whispering the vow. "I place myself under your care, my noble prince."

She started to repeat the words, but he interrupted. "Say it so they can hear you, just like I did."

"I place myself under your care, my noble prince!" She shouted the words, letting her soprano voice ring out clearly in the still night air.

"I pledge you my love and servitude, both in this life and in the one to come."

Again she repeated his words.

"I promise to remain by your side as you destroy any forces that try to tear us apart." She finished the vow as loudly as she had begun it. Maybe someone would hear this lunacy and call for help.

He positioned her at his side, one arm draped across her shoulders. When he looked down at her, his lips curled back in a grin—delighted, proud and completely insane. "Come on," he commanded, "smile and wave to all the people."

He raised his free hand and turned it back and forth, eyes looking out over masses that existed only in his imagination. After a long silence, he smiled down at her, keeping his hand in the air. "Look at that. They're happy for our union."

She nodded, continued to wave and prayed for an end to the madness.

Finally, he lowered his hand, her cue to stop waving, too. The arm he had draped across her shoulder settled at her waist, and he pulled her tightly against him. "I can't believe you're actually mine."

Defiance surged up within. With or without his fantasy ceremony, she would never be his. But she forced herself to submit.

"Smile at them," he ordered. "They're wishing us success on our journey."

"Journey?" New fear stabbed through her. He was taking her somewhere else. She jerked around to look up at him, searching for answers in that detached gaze.

"Yes, our journey to the other side."

*Other side of what?*

Before she could voice the question, fingers dug roughly into her ribs. "I said, smile."

She gritted her teeth and forced her mouth to comply.

"All right," he said, dropping his arm from her shoulders. "They're sending us on our way with their blessing." He looped her arm through his and led her back across the field, along the deteriorated road and toward the bridge.

He was taking her back to the car. Frantic thoughts flitted through her mind, disjointed ideas that she dismissed almost as rapidly as they came. She had to think of something—something a lot less painful than slamming her car into a tree at fifty miles per hour.

She prayed for clarity, some brilliant flash of insight.

She was going to need it.

Kevin drove slowly around Lake Mae, the last of the three lakes in Harmony Grove. As they completed the small loop, Chris's heart sank lower and lower. Missy's car wasn't there, either. Wherever Eugene took her, it wasn't in Harmony Grove.

"Where do you want to go next?"

Kevin was looking at him for direction, but he had none to give. Starting in Harmony Grove gave him something to do, which had helped him hold on to his sanity. For twenty minutes, he had scoured the shores of all three lakes, praying Missy's car would be there. During that time, he had alternated between searching, praying and worrying. BethAnn was evidently doing quite a bit of worrying herself. She sat crowded between him and Kevin and hadn't stopped chewing her nails since getting in the truck.

He let out a heavy sigh. "I feel like we're looking for a needle in a haystack." Polk County had hundreds of lakes. The chances of finding the one Eugene chose were pretty much nonexistent. He put his head in his hands, hopelessness clawing at him. Eugene had taken her right from under his nose. How could he have let it happen? What kind of cop was he, anyway, when he couldn't even protect the woman he loved?

BethAnn put a hand on his shoulder. "They'll find her. Since they're in her car, the cops at least have a good description of the vehicle. In the meantime, we'll just pray that God keeps her safe." The pep talk was likely for herself as much as for him.

"I *have* been praying," he argued. "Since the moment I opened the door and Smudge almost ran me over getting inside."

"If we just had some idea where to go." BethAnn dropped her hand from his shoulder. "Eugene didn't leave any clues in the notes, did he?"

He shook his head. "The notes were just lots of words of adoration and references to fate and his quest and the fact that soon they would be together. Unfortunately, he didn't say where."

Kevin eased the truck to the side of the road. He

had just finished circling the lake for the fourth time. "What about the sketches? Melissa said you guys found a sketchbook in the stable. Any clues there?"

"If there are, they're pretty obscure. Other than a few sketches at the front, the entire book is scenes from some off-the-wall medieval fantasy."

"Can you describe any of the pictures?" Kevin asked.

That he could do. Those images would stay with him until the day he died. "A lot of them had a castle in them, either in the background or worked into the setting itself. In several of the sketches, the two of them stood behind a waist-high wall that seemed to be on a hill or a grassy slope. It looked like they were participating in some ritual or ceremony or something. The last one—"

"Wait," BethAnn interrupted. She flipped on the dome light, picked up her purse and began fishing through it. "Can you draw one of the scenes with this wall you're talking about?"

Chris looked at her with raised eyebrows. "I'm not an artist. I never graduated past stick figures." But as soon as she handed him a pen and a wrinkled grocery list, he began to draw. Within a couple of minutes, he had a crude replica of one of the pictures.

BethAnn snatched the paper from him, gesturing wildly. "I know this place. It's Mary Holland Park. Remember the fort I told you about? Eugene spent a summer in Fort Meade as a kid. If he went to Mary Holland Park then, this is how he would remember it."

Kevin jammed the gas pedal to the floor and squealed onto the pavement, rear end fishtailing for several moments until he gained control. Chris whipped out his cell phone and called nine-one-one. God bless BethAnn. She had figured it out. He was sure of it.

Now if someone could just get there in time.

Fifteen minutes later, Kevin screeched to a halt at the park entrance. The gate was closed, chained and padlocked for the night, and the road was deserted.

A wave of despair washed over Chris, drenching the hope that had burned brightly all the way to Bartow. He'd been so sure Melissa and Eugene would be there, playing the roles depicted in the sketches. "They're not here."

BethAnn reached across him to open the door. "You don't really expect him to park at the main entrance, do you? He might as well put up a neon sign."

He stepped over the gate and started up the tree-lined road at a full run. A deathly stillness had fallen over the park. Pavilions sat empty, concrete benches hard and cold with no happy families to warm them. In the playground, swings swayed gently in the light breeze, lonely and ignored. Even the soccer field was deserted.

But he gave it all just a cursory glance. His focus was on the lakes. And time was running out. Missy and Eugene weren't at the soccer field, so the ceremony at the old fort was over.

There was only one sketch left.

*Dear God, please don't let us be too late.*

# NINETEEN

Eugene straightened his arm and let Melissa's hand fall. Black water kissed the narrow strip of sand inches from the toes of her tennis shoes. Instead of retracing their path over the bridge toward the car, he had led her to the lake.

"Now we make our passage. Hold my hand."

Her gaze shot to his face. He stared straight ahead at the expanse of dark water, his features solemn and unreadable. An image flashed through her mind, and a new wave of terror washed over her. It was the final sketch—she and Eugene standing waist deep in water.

Panic ricocheted in her chest. She shook her head and backed slowly up the bank, hands extended in front of her as if warding off something evil. "No. I'm not going in the water."

Eugene followed, left hand extended, palm up. His right was hidden under his T-shirt, no doubt holding the butt of the gun. "Come on, Melissa. Don't be afraid." The words were more menacing than soothing. "Don't fight it. It's fate. We must make our passage. Two others have already gone ahead. But you, my sweet, will hold the place of highest honor."

She continued to shake her head. Threatening her with death wouldn't lure her into the dark water. Almost all Florida lakes were home to alligators and water moccasins. Just the thought sent icy tendrils of fear slithering up her spine. "I can't do it." Her voice shook. "Let's just go around."

Eugene grabbed her hand and yanked her toward him. "I told you not to fight it." Gone was the soothing tone. If he couldn't coax her into the water, he was going to use brute force. "You don't have a choice. We must make the passage together."

An idea budded, a plan born of sheer desperation. She didn't think it through—there wasn't time. In one swift move, she jerked from his grasp and charged at him, ramming both hands into his shoulders. He hit the ground with a thud. But she didn't see him fall. She was already flying toward the bridge at a full run, shoulders itching for the bullet she expected to explode through her chest.

The earsplitting crack never came. In fact, except for her own fleeing footsteps and frantic gasps for air, the evening was eerily quiet. Then a curse sounded in the distance, followed by a heavy tread. Eugene had begun his pursuit.

She flew across the grassy field, using every ounce of strength she possessed. But he pounded ever closer, until she was sure his hot breath brushed the back of her neck. She couldn't outrun him. She had to outsmart him.

If she suddenly dropped to a crouch, maybe he would somersault over her. The thought flashed through her mind at the speed of light. But in the next millisecond, hands against her shoulder blades sent her hurtling forward, with no time to break her fall. He landed roughly on top of her, knocking the air from her lungs.

The next several moments passed in a blur. One minute she was lying prone, face pressed into the cold, wet grass. The next she was staring at the sky, hands pinned under Eugene's legs as he straddled her. A familiar flavor seeped onto her tongue, coppery and warm. Blood.

She dragged her eyes from the distant heavens and focused on the form kneeling over her—a scene from her worst nightmare. He glared down at her, eyes bulging and lips curled back in a sneer. The fury was no longer restrained. It radiated from him, a force that held her immobile as effectively as his weight pinning her to the ground.

A scream welled up in her throat but never reached her mouth. In one smooth sweep, he raised the gun and slammed its butt into her temple. A searing pain shot through her skull, a red-hot poker being driven into her brain. The accompanying flash momentarily blinded her, then scattered into dozens of tiny swirling lights that slowly drifted downward.

She lifted her gaze to the moon and tried to focus

on its brightness. She couldn't lose consciousness. She must stay alert and fight.

In spite of her best efforts, darkness came anyway. It rolled in from all directions, advancing relentlessly, until even the light of the moon faded to darkest night.

Strong arms encircled her and lifted her from… where? She had no idea. Her head hurt. Actually, it throbbed. But much worse than a throb—more like a tent stake being driven into her temple with every beat of her heart. Then someone was carrying her. She didn't care where, as long as it was a comfortable place to lie down. And she would ask for some headache medicine. Chris would be happy to get her something.

It was Chris who held her, right? Her eyelids were so heavy, she couldn't drag them open. But it had to be Chris. No one else would hold her like that. The arms were strong, the chest firm. She felt protected, safe. But there was something hard and metallic digging into her left hip. If he knew how uncomfortable she was, he would move the offending object. She tried to tell him, but the words wouldn't form. Instead, a moan came from somewhere nearby.

Then there was sloshing. Why was there water all over the floor? And why was Chris walking through it? Couldn't he make it to her bed without walking through all this water? It sloshed and splashed beneath her, then seeped up her fingers and over her hand. It was cold, uncomfortably so. She tried to pull back, but her leaden limbs wouldn't cooperate. Someone needed to drain the water. It was everywhere. Soon it enveloped her feet and her buttocks, and she tried to squirm away from it.

When the cool water reached her chest, the shock jarred her into full consciousness. The lake! Eugene was taking her into the lake!

Terror twisted her gut. As he lowered her into the water, she positioned her feet under her. But she was no match for his strength. He wrapped one hand around her throat and easily pushed her head beneath the surface. He was going to drown her! He claimed that he loved her. Why would he want to kill her?

His earlier words echoed in her mind: *They're wishing us success on our journey...our journey to the other side.* Before it hadn't made sense. Now it did. He wasn't taking her to the other side of the park or county or state. "The journey" was passing from this life to the next. He planned to drown her and somehow kill himself. And whatever warped theology he held promised him they would be together in the life to come.

A massive wave of panic crashed over her, and fragmented thoughts tumbled through her mind, screaming incoherent messages. She flailed her arms and struggled to gain her footing, but he had forced her backward, and no matter how she tried, she couldn't right herself. When she grasped his wrists and tried to pry his hands from her throat, he only tightened his grip.

Then a voice of reason forced its way through the tangled thoughts and demanded attention. Her struggling was only expending valuable energy. She stopped fighting, then drew her legs up and extended them suddenly, ramming her feet into his stomach. His hold loosened just enough for her to twist away from him, and her head burst from the water. She lunged sideways and dove for the shore, frantically sucking in huge gulps of air.

Within moments, talonlike fingers closed on her shoulders, and she fought for all she was worth, jabbing, punching and kicking blindly behind her. But he avoided every blow. He pushed her down and backward, and she hauled in one final, desperate breath before her head plunged beneath the surface.

Fighting was futile now. He stood behind her, well out of reach of her legs and fists. Using the only weapon she had left, she dug her fingernails into the soft skin of his cuticles. He didn't loosen his grip. Instead, the vise tightened, separating muscle, tendon and ligament and penetrating to the bone. Liquid fire shot all the way to her fingertips, and her arms fell away.

*Lord, please send someone.* A glimmer of hope flickered faintly in the far corners of her mind. Maybe someone had stepped out of one of the houses and heard her thrashing around. Not likely.

But at the moment, it was all she had to cling to.

* * *

Chris pushed forward, pressing every ounce of speed from his aching legs. He had found them. They were nothing but silhouettes in the silver light of the moon. But he had no doubt what he saw. Eugene had just carried an unconscious Missy into the lake and now held her beneath the surface. *Dear God, please let us get there in time.*

Maybe he was already too late.

If only he had gone to that lake first. Or if they had split up and he had gone one direction, BethAnn and Kevin the other. Instead, the three of them had run together to the nearest lake. When he scanned its shore, the only shapes rising from the banks were the willows, palms and brush that grew in clumps at the lake's edge. And there was no one in the water. Its dark surface was smooth and unbroken, reflecting the moonlight in a shimmery, silver-white streak.

So he had looked far into the distance, past the canal and the bridge that spanned it, to the lake beyond. And that was when he saw a slight, solitary figure race up the bank. Though she was too far away to identify, he instantly knew. It was Missy. He longed to call out, to tell her he was coming. But he didn't dare.

Then a much larger figure emerged and charged across the grass, quickly closing the gap between them. As he watched, his own legs pumping hard, he willed her to run faster. But within moments, the looming figure had tackled her, pinned her to the ground and knocked her unconscious, effectively ending her struggle.

Now she lay somewhere beneath the surface of the water, life ebbing away with every second that passed.

He skidded to a halt at the edge of the lake, weapon drawn. "Freeze! Police! Hands in the air!"

Eugene raised his head and jerked upright, lifting Melissa from the water and holding her in front of him. The coward was using her as a shield. Chris lunged forward, determined to reach them before Eugene could pull a weapon. But his legs felt as if he were moving through gelatin with a fifty-pound weight attached to each ankle. He was still twenty feet away when Eugene lifted his arm. In his hand was a pistol.

"No, *you* raise *your* hands. And drop the gun. Now!"

Chris slowly released his weapon, letting it fall into the lake with a splash. And that splash represented the death of his last opportunity to save Missy.

He raised both hands and stared at Eugene, mind stalled out. He needed to think of something, something brilliant and persuasive, but his brain was working as efficiently as a computer with a virus, its operating processes shutting down one by one.

Then there was movement beside him, and Kevin stepped forward. "Come on, Eugene, let her go. You don't want to do this."

Kevin became the pistol's new target, and Chris

sent another prayer heavenward. This was his and Missy's battle. He should never have gotten Kevin and BethAnn involved.

"Don't interfere." Eugene's tone held a steely core of determination. "We have to make our passage. And I will spill the blood of anyone who tries to stop us." The gun moved back and forth, always keeping one of them in its sights. "Melissa is mine. I have fought and been deemed worthy. We have made our vows before the gods and all our loyal subjects. What we have done cannot be torn asunder by mere man."

Without lowering the pistol, he took a step back, then another and another, pulling Missy with him. The water at her waist slowly moved up her chest to cover her shoulders. Panic pounded up Chris's spine. Eugene was going to drown her right in front of him. And there was nothing he could do to save her. *Dear God, please help us.*

He glanced over at Kevin, silently pleading with him to do something, and hope spiked through him. Beyond Kevin, near the pavilions, was the answer to his prayer—one shadowed figure and another and another…five in all. The police. Maybe even a SWAT team.

Relief clashed with rising panic. They would be there in seconds.

But what would Eugene do when he saw them?

Melissa continued to suck in huge gulps of air. Every cell in her body screamed for oxygen. Eugene held her pinned against him, which was probably a good thing. Otherwise, she would have collapsed and sunk beneath the surface. Her bones had turned to chalk, her muscles to gelatin.

When Eugene had suddenly hoisted her from the water moments earlier, confusion had tumbled over relief. Had he changed his mind? Was he going to let her live? It wasn't until she'd wiped the water from her eyes and looked toward the shore that she'd understood. Chris had come for her. So had BethAnn and Kevin.

But the gun was no longer tucked into the waistband of Eugene's pants. It was drawn, cocked and ready to fire. And it was leveled on Chris. Her heart almost stopped. She had pleaded with God to send someone. Was that prayer going to cost Chris and her friends their lives?

As Eugene pulled her deeper, farther and farther from Chris, determination coursed through her. It couldn't end like this, with Eugene winning while Chris, Kevin and BethAnn helplessly looked on. She clawed and pinched and delivered several ineffective elbow jabs to the muscled abdomen against her back. But Eugene only tightened his hold, cutting off what little air she had left. Icy water splashed against her face and into her eyes.

She stopped her struggling and met Chris's gaze across the expanse of murky water. His face was shrouded in shadow. But each detail was etched in her imagination, and she clung to the image as if it were her lifeline. Did he have any idea how much she loved him? Probably not. And she would regret it all the way to her grave.

Eugene took another step back and another, until the water covered her mouth. She tilted her head back, just enough to still be able to breathe, and without breaking eye contact with Chris, mouthed the words, "I love you." Then she touched her fingers lightly to her lips and angled them toward him in the gesture of a blown kiss. But it was too little, too late. She had passed up every opportunity to tell him how she felt. Suddenly all her reasons for guarding her heart seemed petty and insignificant.

"Freeze!" The single word rang sharp and clear, jarring her to her toes, and she scanned the bank, searching for its source. Five figures approached, clad in black, weapons drawn. Eugene must have been as shocked as she was, because for a fraction of a second, the steel band loosened, the miracle she had prayed for. She twisted free, dropped beneath the surface and swam for all she was worth. Her lungs burned, her arms ached and her legs began to cramp. But she pushed beyond the bounds of her endurance and made for the shore, praying all the while that Eugene would be subdued before she had to come up for air.

The instant her head broke the surface, her blood turned to ice in her veins. Screams pierced the stillness of the night, high-pitched wails of agony that rattled her bones and shredded her nerves. Someone was hurt. She wiped the water from her eyes and searched the bank, disoriented. Her blind swim had taken her far to the right. When she found Chris, Kevin and BethAnn, she heaved a sigh of relief. They were fine.

Eugene wasn't. He was bent at the waist, left hand pressed against his right shoulder, sending up a series of shrieks that didn't die until two officers led him out of the water. Then something snapped, and the howls of pain became sobs of despair.

"It wasn't supposed to happen like this," he wailed. He dropped to his knees on the grassy bank. "She was mine. Now everything is ruined."

The officers pulled him to his feet and half dragged, half carried him toward the waiting patrol car. Melissa turned from the spectacle on shore to look at Chris. He was already rushing clumsily toward her, lunging, diving, swimming. Her knees buckled, and darkness began to roll in. She felt herself falling...deeper...deeper....

Her face never touched the water. Instead, strong arms encircled her, lifting her from the lake, holding her tightly.

And she lost herself in the safety of those arms.

Because this time they belonged to Chris.

# TWENTY

Chris reached the hospital elevator just as the doors opened. An older gentleman stepped in, then turned toward him, smiling. "Which floor?"

"Four. Thank you." He grinned at the old man. "I guess I got a little carried away."

He had gone into the hospital gift shop planning to get a card and some flowers. He came out with both. A mixed bouquet of roses, daisies, lilies and some kind of small lavender flowers occupied one hand. The other held the card—along with a heart-shaped box of chocolates and a small weight connected by a ribbon to a get-well-soon balloon. A teddy bear was tucked under one arm.

"She must be one special lady."

"That's an understatement."

The elevator door opened, and he nodded to the man and stepped into the hall. Missy's room was three-quarters of the way down on the left. He had visited her briefly last night. But by the time they finished running tests and moved her there from the emergency room, it was almost midnight, far past visiting hours. As much as he hated to leave her, he had to agree with the nurse—she needed her rest.

From the moment he left the hospital, time had passed at a snail's pace. One scene played over and over in his mind—her head tilted back, face awash with the silver glow of the moon, lips moving in a silent "I love you." And just in case he wasn't sure what he saw, she followed it with a kiss.

Would she still feel the same way in the stark light of a new day? Now that the danger was over and she had her whole life ahead of her, would she still be willing to drop her guard and let him in? Or would the walls go right back up?

He approached her room and stood in the doorway for several moments, not yet alerting her of his presence. The TV was on, its volume hardly above a whisper. But her attention wasn't on the screen. Her face was turned away, toward the window. Morning sunlight streamed in, bathing her in its warm glow. The back of her bed was raised to an almost upright position, and she sat unmoving, hair flowing in waves over her shoulder and down her arm.

Emotion surged up from within, a love so powerful it almost took his breath away. He had come so close to losing her. Another two or three minutes was all it would have taken. He drew in a shaky breath and, for the hundredth time since holding her against him, wet and unconscious, he thanked God for sparing her life.

He cleared his throat and stepped into the room. A lingering pensiveness marked her features for just a moment before being replaced by a bright smile.

"How do you feel?"

"A little stiff. Ready to go home. Happy to be alive." Her gaze dropped to her hands, folded in her lap. "Terrible that I blamed Dennis. Mrs. Johnson will never forgive me."

"She already has. I went over and talked to her this morning, and she fully understood. All the clues pointed to Dennis. She said to tell you not to feel bad about it."

"Well, I definitely owe him an apology, and somehow I don't think he's going to be as forgiving as his grandmother."

"Well, hopefully this will cheer you up." He placed the bouquet, chocolates and balloon weight on her bedside table and handed her the card and the bear.

"Couldn't decide what to get, so you got it all?" She grinned up at him.

He returned her smile. "Something like that."

She hugged the teddy bear and opened the card. When she had finished reading it, she looked up at him, eyes moist. "Thank you."

Doubt began to chew away at his optimism. He had searched until he found a card that told her exactly how he felt. And he was pretty sure he knew what *she* felt. He had seen it in her gaze last night. How could he convince her to trust him with her love?

"Any idea when they're going to let you go home?"

"The doctor said he's going to release me later today. Other than a concussion and a rather large bump on the side of my head, he said I'm doing all right. Pretty good news, considering the circumstances."

"It sure is." He sat in the chair next to her bed. "Well, *I* got some good news this morning, too. The detectives investigating my case haven't found Donna, but the paper trail led them to an offshore account. A lot of the money is gone, but there's still enough that if I put it on the mortgage, I should be able to get a new loan for the rest."

"That's awesome. See, God really does answer prayer."

"I have no doubt about that. Last night He was working overtime." He fell silent as memories bombarded him—the fear, the anguish, the total sense of helplessness. "Things were pretty grim there for a while. After all I had done to protect you, it looked like I was going to lose you anyway."

"I know. And all I kept thinking about was how I was going to die without ever telling you how I feel." Her gaze again dropped to her hands.

His heart rolled over, and he held his breath, waiting for her to continue. *Say the words.* "And how is that?" he prodded.

For several moments, she didn't respond. When she finally lifted her eyes to meet his, they glistened with meaning. And he knew. Even without the words, he knew.

She drew in a deep breath. "I love you. I don't believe I really ever stopped loving you. I was so hurt and angry and didn't want to forgive you. And then when I found out that Adrianne had lied, that you hadn't been unfaithful, I was afraid. I was afraid that, as deeply as I loved you, if you ever left, it would destroy me. And I just wasn't willing to take that risk. But the moment I saw you unconscious in your truck the day of your accident, I realized something. I would rather risk a broken heart than face an empty future without you."

He pushed the table aside and pulled his chair right next to her bed so he could take her hands. "What can I do to show you how much I love you, to assure you that I'll never let anything come between us ever again?"

She squeezed his hands, a warm smile lighting her eyes. "You already have."

"No, there's one more thing I can do." He stood, pushed the chair aside with his leg and got down on one knee. "Missy, will you marry me?"

She pulled him closer, until she could wrap her arms around him and pull him closer still. "Yes," she whispered against his neck. "I would love to marry you."

For several moments, she held him tightly. Then her hands moved to cup his face, holding it about six inches from her own. He had said he wouldn't push.

He had promised her that the next time he kissed her, it would be initiated by her.

And it was.

\* \* \* \* \*

*If you enjoyed this story by Carol Post,
be sure to check out the other books this month
from Love Inspired Suspense!*

Dear Reader,

Thank you for reading *Midnight Shadows,* my first published book. I hope you enjoyed it. Melissa and Chris were fun characters for me to write, because I could empathize with both of them. Forgiveness and trust are so important in a relationship, but aren't always easy to achieve. When others hurt us, it's sometimes easier to hang on to the hurt and put up walls than to work through the pain and let it go. And that's true no matter where we are in our spiritual walk.

In *Midnight Shadows,* Melissa had a relationship with the Lord, but she had to deal with unforgiveness. Chris believed in an all-powerful but disinterested God who has no concern for our daily problems. Throughout the story, he grows into a relationship with the Lord and finds that God isn't the distant force he once thought. In Melissa's words, "He's close and personal and cares about every aspect of our lives." According to Matthew 10:30, He has the hairs on our heads numbered. You can't get more close and personal than that! God calls us "friend" and wants an intimate relationship with each of us. And that is my prayer for you—that God will make Himself real and that you will experience an ever-deepening friendship with Him.

For more information about me and my books, you can check out my website at caroljpost.com, or email me at caroljpost@gmail.com. I love to connect with readers!

May God richly bless you.
*Carol J. Post*

# Questions for Discussion

1. Melissa has taken care of herself since she was a child and has difficulty leaning on others. Can you relate to her? Why or why not?

2. Throughout most of the story, Chris views God as a distant, all-powerful force who has no interest in the concerns of individuals, while Melissa believes God is "close and personal and cares about every aspect of our lives." What are some ways to reach a person who holds Chris's impersonal view of God?

3. At the beginning of the story, Melissa thinks she has no hard feelings toward Chris, but seeing him again brings all the anger and resentment bubbling to the surface. What scripture passages could she find healing in reading? Are there any wrongs that you find unforgivable? What are some benefits of living without bitterness?

4. Chris regrets letting Melissa go five years earlier and not spending more time with his father. Some regrets in life are inevitable, but what are some ways people can eliminate the likelihood of regrets later on?

5. When Chris believes he has lost Melissa and finds out that he is on the verge of bankruptcy,

he feels his life is spiraling out of control. Have you ever had adverse circumstances hit one after the other? How did you cope?

6. Melissa believed for five years that Chris was unfaithful, then learned she was wrong. Have you ever believed something bad about someone then found out you were wrong? How did you feel?

7. When Melissa finds someone has been coming into her house, she believes her stalker is Dennis, which seems confirmed when they find the sketchbook. She doesn't realize she's wrong until Eugene gets into her car. At what point did you know her stalker was Eugene?

8. BethAnn is a true friend, always ready to lend support and encouragement, but not afraid to give Melissa a push when she needs it. What special friends do you have who have made a difference in your life? What are some qualities that you look for in a true friend?

9. Chris's mother abandoned him and his father, and Melissa's father was unfaithful to her mother. How did these experiences affect them in their relationship with each other? How have your childhood experiences shaped your life as an adult?

10. Mrs. Johnson is a sort of grandmother figure to Melissa. Have you had anyone in your life who,

though not related, stepped into a grandmotherly or grandfatherly role? Is there a younger person you know who could benefit from that type of a relationship with you?

11. Melissa has responded to the hurts she has experienced by building protective walls around her heart. Is that something you can relate to? How can being guarded hurt a relationship? Do you believe a certain amount of vulnerability is necessary for true intimacy? Why or why not?

12. When in the story does Melissa first realize the depth of her feelings for Chris? When did you first fall in love with your significant other? Were you willing to admit it at the time?

13. Even though Chris is a new Christian, he prays for Melissa's safety and for his business, and God answers both of those prayers. When have you prayed for something recently and God answered that prayer? Did that help to strengthen your faith? How do you react when God seems slow to answer, or his answer is no? Does that shake your faith?

14. Chris is a detective, and as soon as he discovers that Melissa is in danger, he feels the need to protect her, even though he is on leave. As the story progresses, he risks his own life to keep her safe.

What do you think makes someone a hero? Who are the heroes in your life?

15. Although Melissa was resistant, Chris wanted her to call on him if she was in trouble. Who do you call on when you need help? Encouragement? Advice? A shoulder to cry on? Spiritual counsel?

# LARGER-PRINT BOOKS!

## GET 2 FREE LARGER-PRINT NOVELS PLUS 2 FREE MYSTERY GIFTS

*Love Inspired®*

## SUSPENSE
### RIVETING INSPIRATIONAL ROMANCE

### Larger-print novels are now available...

# *Love Inspired*®

## HEARTWARMING INSPIRATIONAL ROMANCE

Contemporary,
inspirational romances
with Christian characters
facing the challenges
of life and love
in today's world.

**AVAILABLE IN REGULAR
AND LARGER-PRINT FORMATS.**

For exciting stories that reflect traditional values,
visit:
*www.ReaderService.com*

# *ReaderService*.com

## Manage your account online!

- Review your order history
- Manage your payments
- Update your address

## Enjoy all the features!

- Reader excerpts from any series
- Respond to mailings and special monthly offers
- Discover new series available to you
- Browse the Bonus Bucks catalog
- Share your feedback

*Visit us at:*
## ReaderService.com

RS13